Gently then, Barron broke the kiss

"There," he breathed. "The primitive may have a limited appeal for some, but I think you're an exception to that rule." His lips twisted into a mocking smile.

"How dare you!" Belinda's voice shook with hopelessly mixed emotions. "You're the most hateful arrogant man I've ever met!" His answer was to bring his lips crushingly down on her own again, and to her shame Belinda responded rapturously.

At once he let her go, giving a short unamused laugh. "You're so different, aren't you? You wouldn't barter your body for anything. No!" he sneered, "You'd give it away—"

"No!" Belinda's voice was harsh, insulting. "You're the last person I'd give *anything* to!"

"We'll see," he whispered menacingly. "You've taken on more than you can handle, mixing with me."

WELCOME
TO THE WONDERFUL WORLD
OF *Harlequin Presents*

Interesting, informative and entertaining,
each Harlequin Romance portrays an appealing
and original love story. With a varied array
of settings, we may lure you on an African safari,
to a quaint Welsh village, or an exotic Riviera
location—anywhere and everywhere that adventurous
men and women fall in love.

As publishers of Harlequin Romances, we're
extremely proud of our books. Since 1949,
Harlequin Enterprises has built its publishing
reputation on the solid base of quality and
originality. Our stories are the most popular
paperback romances sold in North America; every
month, six new titles are released and sold at
nearly every book-selling store in Canada and the
United States.

A free catalogue listing all Harlequin Romances
can be yours by writing to the

HARLEQUIN READER SERVICE,
(In the U.S.) 1440 South Priest Drive, Tempe, AZ 85281
(In Canada) Stratford, Ontario, Canada N5A 6W2

We sincerely hope you enjoy reading
this Harlequin Romance.

Yours truly,

THE PUBLISHERS
Harlequin Romances

SANDRA CLARK

the wolf man

Harlequin Books

TORONTO • LONDON • LOS ANGELES • AMSTERDAM
SYDNEY • HAMBURG • PARIS • STOCKHOLM • ATHENS • TOKYO

Harlequin Presents edition published July 1982
ISBN 0-373-10514-2

Original hardcover edition published in 1982
by Mills & Boon Limited

CHAPTER ONE

THE little four-seater aircraft dropped suddenly, lurched to one side, then quickly began to climb again. Reassuringly the young pilot grinned at Belinda. 'Nervous?' he shouted above the roar of the engines. White-faced, she shook her head. She remembered a saying from somewhere: 'There are old pilots, and there are bold pilots, but there are no old, bold pilots'. She darted a sidelong glance at the man beside her. There was no doubt that the pilot with the curly reddish hair and humorous blue eyes sitting next to her was bold. He wasn't exactly old either. She gripped the side of the bucket seat and tried to concentrate on the view through the window.

They had passed the last few stunted trees on the ragged edges of the vast pine forest which had seemed an hour ago to stretch endlessly beneath them, and now below was the naked tundra interlaced with countless wind-scudded lakes and tarns. In the late afternoon haze they seemed to form just one huge lake, and the land itself seemed to resemble no more than a scattering of innumerable little islands.

Soon they would be approaching that region of Northern Canada called the Barren Grounds, and as Belinda took in the grey rock and scrub, and the icy slash of green-grey water, her blue eyes became troubled. Conversation was impossible above the noise of the engine and there were so many things she wanted to ask.

Some time ago the pilot had taken off his moccasins, and his fur-lined parka was slung carelessly to one side in the cockpit. The warmth from the engine was beginning to have some effect on the bitter cold, but Belinda snuggled down in her pink quilted jacket and tried to resign herself without success to the noise, the hair-raising flight of the plane, and worse, the harshness of the inhospitable country below them.

Silly, to have doubts about a little air shuttle between Paulatuk and the settlement, she told herself. The Eskimos and the whites who lived in this frozen country used light aircraft as casually as she would use her own little car back home. Despite the accident, she would still think nothing of buzzing off somewhere for the day as the fancy took her. She was letting the strange bleakness of the landscape drain her natural adventurousness. At times like these I need to give myself a good talking to, she admonished, under her breath, as the plane bucked again. Why, if it wasn't because I wanted to be here, I'd still be at home in England, trapped in the same old dull routine.

'Well, penny for them!' The pilot raised his voice above the roar of the engine.

Belinda shook herself. She grinned up at him sheepishly. 'Daydreaming,' she said. 'I was just thinking, this is a change from the same old dull routine back home.'

The pilot shot her a quizzical glance. 'What's the old routine back home, then?' he grinned.

Belinda hesitated. 'I guess I'm a sort of very junior assistant in a university,' she told him.

She tried to make it sound boring. But in reality she had to admit she enjoyed her job as assistant researcher to the professor of linguistics at an English university, and not only because Derek was one of the dishiest men she knew.

She let her mind go over the last few weeks in an attempt to distract it from the endless view of rock and scrub below. She still felt a flicker of pride when she recalled the day she had been called into Derek's study. He was standing by the window when she came in, and turned with that special smile as she burst breathlessly through the door. Married, with two sons almost as old as

Belinda herself, he had successfully resisted the temptation to be unfaithful to his wife. He was not the sort of man to take advantage of his position as head of a large department in this popular university. He was no philanderer, though sometimes he idly speculated on the surprising fact that the girl students seemed to get prettier each year. Then one day Belinda had arrived, a fresh-faced undergraduate, straight from boarding school, and his idle speculations were swept away in the surge of a new and very disturbing emotion. She was a lovely girl, tall and blonde, with a wistful, piquant beauty which belied a sharpness of mind and a rather belligerent determination which Derek found wholly delightful. Carefully, and still faithfully, he allowed her into his more private fantasies, but she would have been destined to remain in the realm of unfulfilled longings as a distant and unattainable distraction if fate had not taken a tragic hand in the matter.

Belinda's father was a minor official in the Diplomatic Service, and one summer's day, while he was driving back through Europe with his wife, his car had skidded uncontrollably, and, as it proved, fatally, on a remote mountain pass. Belinda was stunned by the news. An only child, she turned overnight from being a bright, vivacious girl, into a pale and depressed shadow of her former self. It suddenly seemed to her that all her efforts to gain a degree had gone for nought.

Derek had shared the pain of her loss. He had held her close, tenderly but briefly, on hearing of the accident, but from his position as her professor it seemed there was little he could do without compromising his own status. Irresistibly he felt himself sharing more and more deeply in her anguish as the days of that dreadful summer came and went. For a time he had made himself available just to listen and to wipe away the tears as she slowly came to terms with the fact that she was now alone in the world, and, with only token resistance, he had felt himself being drawn into a deep and possibly dangerous commitment.

He had had to use every ounce of self-control in order not to exploit the situation, for he knew that in her grief Belinda was beginning to lean on him, to regard him as someone special, a friend, a father figure perhaps, an attachment of a romantic sort, who could perhaps fill the aching void in her life, and he in his turn longed guiltily to become more than just her academic mentor and guide.

Although these unaccustomed sensations had filled him with a strange joy he was too honourable a man to put his desires into action. He loved his wife, he loved his children. But for Belinda and the maelstrom of emotions she aroused, there would have been no ripple to disturb the orderly calm on the surface of his life. How the relationship would have worked itself out, he had no idea, but a reprieve was granted by, of all things, the board of postgraduate studies.

That august body had decided to make available certain funds, which, it advised, should be spent on sending a researcher to complete an essential study of the fast-disappearing language of a small and nomadic tribal group who inhabited the central region of the North-West Territories. Derek, as appointing professor for this interesting assignment, had forced himself to give serious consideration to the qualifications of the other researchers. All men, any one of them would have jumped at the chance to carry out the work, and there was much inter-necine warfare conducted in the usually hushed confines of the junior staff common room. But it had to be Belinda. It was a heaven-sent opportunity to get her out of his system. Six months apart and he knew he would have fought the temptation and won. Besides, he told himself as he looked at that lovely mouth now curved in an ex-pectant smile, the girl needed to get away from this place, a change of scene would do wonders to dispel the still paralysing bouts of depression she occasionally still suffered six months after the tragedy. It was true, too, that she needed to get down to some practical research at this stage of her career, in order to add to her chances of getting a junior academic post later on. She had herself to support now, he argued, and this would be an ideal way to acquire incalculable experience.

Briefly he told her of the proposal, outlining the main reasons why she should not hesitate to seize the opportunity with both hands. The university would pay all expenses for three months, he told her, and, he went on, before she could raise a protest, she would fly out to Canada in two weeks' time, make contact with a Professor Neilson at a Toronto college, who was an expert on Eskimo languages and would give her letters of introduction to one of the leading fur traders in the North. She would then stay at the trading post long enough to establish contact with the group under study. Armed with tape recorder and plenty of notebooks and common sense, she would have the rare opportunity to further the cause of linguistic research in this restricted but important field.

He raised one eyebrow quizzically. 'You don't look overjoyed at the honour about to be conferred on you,' he said drily.

Belinda spread her hands. 'What do I know of the Eskimo phylum?' she demanded. 'Next to nothing. Do you want me to make a complete fool of myself?'

He regarded her with a wry smile of amusement. 'I wouldn't let you go if I thought you were going to make a fool of yourself. If you make a fool of yourself, you make a fool of the department, and that wouldn't do our egos any good in the Dominion, would it?' He moved one or two papers about on his desk. 'You have one of the best degrees in the department,' he told her. 'And I'm not one of these professors who likes to waste his best brains in simple pen-pushing duties. Here's a challenge for you, I think you're worthy of it.'

He gave her a brief rundown on the tribe whose language she was to study. 'They number probably no more than a hundred people, men, women and children,' he told her, 'but owing to the changes in education, health and economic conditions in the last decade and the government's strenuous efforts to retrain them, they are beginning to give up their old nomadic way of life as hunters and trappers and to settle in the new townships which are springing up around the mining, canning and radar communication centres around the Arctic Circle.'

'It sounds cold,' Belinda commented.

'You'll survive it,' he replied, looking her up and down. She lifted her chin. 'Would I want to?' she sparred.

Derek let his glance linger, almost without realising it, on that slim body which he so longed to explore. Belinda bit her lip. When Derek looked at her like that she could forget he was supposed to be her boss. Angrily she glared back at him, and he pulled himself together.

'Before these people are assimilated entirely into the modern world some record of their language and customs has to be made. Several Norse words are in everyday use, for instance——' He stopped. It was difficult to talk seriously now, when every minute they were together seemed precious. 'In short, a more detailed knowledge of how their language has developed will give the sociologist something to chew over, as well as giving us something interesting to bite on too.'

He finished with a wry smile, pleased to have got so swiftly over the problematical details of the assignment and on to the safe ground of academic detail, but Belinda was less easily won over.

'I know nothing,' she repeated. 'Nothing!'

'Don't tell me you know nothing when you've just spent three years on the taxpayers' money ostensibly studying,' he told her severely. Belinda's chin rose. 'Your recent work on a standard orthography will give you a sufficient background to be able to make some very useful contributions in this area.' He regarded her solemnly over the expanse of his desk. She still made mild protests, but he ignored her objections point blank. 'There are two main languages in the Eskimo stock, as you know,' he went on, turning to gaze out of the window where in the summer term the students and in particular Belinda had disported themselves so distractingly. 'There's Impik and Yupik and innumerable dialects based on these two. You will only concern yourself with Impik,' he told her.

Belinda heaved a sigh of relief. Her knowledge of either root was scanty, but the more she thought about Derek's proposition the more excited by it she became. It would be a real challenge, something to get her teeth into at least, and maybe something to wipe away the pain of the last few months.

She leaned forward, forgetting her earlier objections, her blonde hair brushing her cheek, her eyes alight with interest though guarded, lips moist and slightly parted. Trying to keep the note of interest out of her voice, she said coolly: 'Well, it will certainly be an experience, if I decide to say "yes", that is. It sounds like quite a challenge in its way. I mean, to live with people from a totally different culture. It might be fun. Who knows?' she added flippantly.

Derek frowned a little. 'Don't think it's going to be easy,' he told her testily. 'I suppose I ought to warn you, these people are nomadic and have deliberately kept themselves away from white civilisation, and indeed from the members of their own Eskimo nation too. They're not noted for their approachability. They may refuse to have anything to do with you.'

'In which case,' said Belinda quickly, 'my whole journey will have been pointless.'

'Quite,' he replied drily, then a brief smile broke across his face. 'I know you won't let me down when I tell you how I have to go cap in hand to raise any finance whatsoever for the department. If we make a mess of this one it'll make any future fund-raising attempts even more difficult to pull off. But I know you'll let nothing stand in your way.'

The boost to her confidence was just what she needed. 'I'd certainly hate to see all your efforts go to waste, Derek,' she said, with a tilt of her chin. She wasn't a fool. She knew why Derek was so eager to give her the opportunity. She too welcomed it, for she had been half afraid of the emotions he was beginning to arouse in her, realising that it was mainly out of weakness that she had begun to succumb to his mature charm. She smiled reassuringly. 'You can trust me,' she told him. 'I've never let you down yet.'

'Still boasting about your double first?' he teased.

A shadow crossed her face. 'It was all due to you, wasn't it? If you hadn't lent me a shoulder to cry on when I was all to pieces——' She paused. She knew she was treading dangerous ground.

After the initial shock of finding herself an orphan she had become powerfully aware of Derek, his dry humour, his warmth and concern for her. She had no intention of stealing another woman's husband, but if circumstances had been different, she would have found it hard to resist him. He was, after all, a man in his prime, attractive, and in his own field, distinguished too. As it was, she was determined to learn all over again how to stand on her own two feet. This new assignment was just the shot in the arm she needed in order to launch the new, independent image she was determined to create for herself.

It was later as she walked away from Derek's study that it dawned on her how lucky she was to have been chosen to make such an incredible journey. The men will be livid, she thought, but I'm certainly as well qualified as any of them. She smiled suddenly. To be free from the daily desk routine, the pen-pushing as Derek had disparagingly called it. To be free to walk alone beneath an open sky not knowing what the day was going to bring! Above all, to be free from memories of recent pain. The thought itself was like a tonic. She looked ironically at the white-capped lake below as the little plane flew steadily northwards. Well, I'm free from routine now, she thought grimly. The plane pitched and rolled as if to taunt her.

The previous day she had flown to Paulatuk on a scheduled inter-city flight. There was a thirty-room school there and the Eskimo children were flown in from the outlying districts at the beginning of every term. But in the place she was now heading for there was no school, no industrial complex, just a trading post at a junction between two rivers.

Soon the plane began to lose altitude. The pilot shouted something to her and she strained her eyes in the direction he was pointing. Sure enough, there on the horizon were signs of a settlement of some kind.

As they approached she began to make out the shapes of several buildings, and when they drew even closer she could see a long single-storey timber building together with several smaller frame houses set along the edge of a muddy track. There was a stand of sitka pines and beyond that a wide expanse of leaden-coloured lake.

There was no snow. Belinda turned to Chuck, mouthing her surprise above the roar of the engine. Unable to make out what she was saying, he merely grinned in reply before pushing the nose of the plane down and taking them in close over the tops of the buildings. He buzzed the settlement once, then turned back and headed in to land. Belinda, tingling with a mixture of apprehension and eagerness, zipped up her jacket and leaned forward in excitement to catch her first glimpse of her new base. Already figures were beginning to appear from out of the buildings. They were looking up into the sky and one or two children waved and broke away from the rest of the group to come running and shouting along the edge of the runway. At least Belinda assumed that the stony track marked out by blue petrol drums was the runway. It looked more like a cart track. Soon the Anson was bumping along it and when it seemed as if they were about to crash into the little stand of pines, it jerked to a stop and suddenly everything was very quiet.

Chuck turned to her. 'All passengers for Two Rivers International Airport proceed to Customs.'

'You didn't say anything about safety belts,' said Belinda drily, but then she turned to him with a delighted grin spreading prettily over her face. 'This is really, really it, then?' she cried. 'Journey's end?'

'If it's the Nasaq you want to meet up with,' replied Chuck, laconically, 'it'll be more like journey's beginning.' Without elaborating he swung her gear easily across the back of the seat, opened the door and jumped athletically to the ground. A smiling group of dark-haired, golden-skinned children, all clad warmly in fur-lined parkas and leggings, clustered round the young pilot. They hung on to the sleeves of his jacket, chattering and giggling, until Belinda came to the door of the aircraft. Then at the sight of her blonde hair and stylish European winter sports clothes they stared open-mouthed until Chuck, the grin never leaving his face, made way for her. She swung lightly down into his arms. For a moment she was powerfully aware of the lean young body pressed against her own, and by the way his hands lingered on her body and his eyes held hers before setting her down on the runway, she knew he too had felt a physical magnetism pass between them.

'I'll bring your gear,' he said gruffly, turning quickly back to the cabin.

For a confused moment Belinda stood looking round her. There was really nothing very much to see. She was conscious all at once of the endless plateau lifting and falling imperceptibly to a distant horizon which circled the settlement without a break. No chimneys, no buildings broke the promise of an unending solitude.

Belinda was already a little disorientated by the last few days—the air flight across the Atlantic was her very

first time out of Europe, and then there had been the day
and night spent on the campus of the university, meeting
her contact for the assignment. It had been a sort of half-
way house between the academic world she was used to,
and the more down-to-earth world of hunters and trappers
of the far north which she was entering. The people she
had met on campus were much like academic types anywhere, but they had an added air of huskiness in both
physique and clothing style that struck strangely to eyes
that were accustomed only to English manners and
fashions.

The man Derek had called old Neilson turned out to
be a youngish-looking fifty-year-old professor, with rugged
good looks which his dark horn-rimmed spectacles, though
giving him a professorial air, did little to disguise. The
sort of man, Belinda thought to herself, who is equally at
home in the seminar room or on the farm. A party of sorts
had developed later, after he had given her exhaustive
lists of words and orthographical memoranda, and she
had had a pleasant evening, buoyed up by everyone's
enthusiasm and encouragement for the long journey still
ahead of her. Almost reluctantly she had boarded another
plane to take her yet further north.

Then after an overnight stop at one of the larger settlements, there had been one more flight, and here she was.

Later, when she wrote her first letter to Derek, she was
to describe how the planes had got smaller and smaller as
she progressed northwards, as if, she whimsically told him,
she was like Alice in Wonderland, growing larger and
larger as time went on.

Now she seemed to tower over the group of Eskimo
women who had followed their offspring on to the runway
and surged around her with smiles of welcome lighting up
their almost oriental-looking faces. None of them seemed
to be much over five feet tall, and she became suddenly
very conscious of her five feet six inches, like being a teen-
ager all over again, selfconscious and awkward in her new

height—also, she realised, sort of speechless too, as she failed to make any sense of what anybody was saying. She glanced helplessly back at Chuck. He was already swinging the rest of her baggage down out of the cabin and was striding over the stony track towards the long frame building she had spotted from the sky. The group of Eskimos, still chattering and laughing, followed at his heels, while in the doorway of the building stood an elderly couple, smiles of welcome on their faces.

Amidst all the confusion and noisy excitement of their arrival only one figure remained aloof.

Sitting on a crate at the end of the runway was a motionless figure in traditional Eskimo gear of deerskins and fur boots. Man or woman, Belinda couldn't tell at such a distance, for the fur-lined hood of a parka was pulled up against the biting wind which came in from the lake.

Automatically Belinda drew out a pink woollen hat from her pocket and put it on, leaving just a fringe of blonde hair showing.

The Eskimo women had turned back and were gesticulating and saying something among themselves, then, obviously fascinated by this newcomer, they followed closely behind her, chatting all the while. Belinda smiled in mystification when one of the women had spoken directly to her in the not unattractive dialect of the region, but when the woman put out a hand to touch the blonde hair which showed underneath her hat, Belinda guessed what they were chatting about. She had nodded and smiled, like any tourist anywhere in the world, and smiled back, and pointed to their own straight raven-black locks. They had all laughed again and nodded approvingly, and one of the women squeezed Belinda's arm in a sudden show of friendship.

'Blondes are a rare commodity around these parts.' A deep drawling voice made her look up with a start.

Chuck, almost at the building by now, had been

followed, after a moment's hesitation, by the group of women and children, so that Belinda suddenly found herself almost alone on the tarmac.

She was looking up into the face of a white man. Evidently he had left his vantage point on the crate and, with the hood of his jacket still partly obscuring his face, he was standing only a couple of feet behind her. He must have moved very quickly and very silently to have reached the group without her noticing him. Now she could see a pair of blue eyes like chipped ice smiling sardonically into her own. She shivered. They were the bluest, the coldest eyes she had seen in a long time.

The man's glance swept over her body appraisingly and a half smile played about his lips. She had an overwhelming sense of a formidable personality. But for his almost scruffy Eskimo-style attire, he could have passed for a figure of some authority. Unaccountably she felt a little knot of fear in the pit of her stomach, but it was soon followed by a resurgence of the Belinda Derek had first known. She glared at the man with ill-concealed antagonism. How dared this total stranger suggest she was a commodity? How dared he look at her in that blatantly appraising way, as if examining some prospective purchase? Two spots of colour showed in her cheeks. She knew she had now set foot in a man's world and that things would be tough, but so far she had been unaware of any chauvinism in the men she had met. Was this a foretaste of what was to come? With an effort she bit back the angry words which had come readily to her lips.

The man shot a sardonic look at the fashionable quilted jacket she was wearing. Belinda noticed the direction of his glance and looked hurriedly down. She had thought it looked practical as well as attractive in the winter sports boutique where she had bought it in England, but now, in this tough environment, it seemed suddenly frivolous and not at all the good buy she had first imagined. The man's contemptuous look confirmed the misgivings.

'What's this stuff?' He caught hold of her cuff between his thumb and forefinger.

'Ciré nylon,' answered Belinda defensively.

The stranger gave a short, hard laugh. 'Synthetic junk,' he scoffed. 'Western man hasn't yet invented the material that can outdo caribou skin for lightness, warmth and watertightness,' he told her. 'Should you ever think of going gallivanting off into the wilds, you'll have to get yourself properly kitted out.' He grinned, and his eyes gleamed wolfishly.

Belinda merely glared at him. His effrontery left her speechless. She gave a disdainful shrug and turned away without speaking.

She half expected the man to follow, but he had fallen silent, and when she reached the building and glanced back, sure he was still watching, he had turned on his heel and was already walking off down the track which, she could see, led directly to the lake.

She shrugged and turned her attention to the welcoming committee on the porch. A grey-haired, sweet-faced woman of about fifty came forward with outstretched arms. She took Belinda's hands in her own and drew her towards the house. 'Come on, Mac, you booby, give our visitor a big hello,' she said over her shoulder, and a tall, rather stooped but neatly bearded man stood talking to Chuck with his arms folded, a warm smile lighting up his face as Belinda approached.

Chuck cuffed him on the arm. 'Mac Macdonald, I've never known you struck dumb before!' He turned to Belinda. 'Chief of Two Rivers Trading Post. And I'll be the first to admit he runs a tight little outfit around here.'

Mac put out a large gnarled hand which almost swamped Belinda's delicate white one, then without releasing it he took over from his wife and led the girl inside the house.

'O.K., Chuck me boy, you can go now,' he threw over his shoulder with a wicked grin. 'I can see why you've kept this one quiet—you might have told me you were bringing a little girl out for me.'

'You don't get rid of me as quickly as that,' replied Chuck, hastening after them. 'Besides, I'm a better catch than you. I'm not already spoken for.'

'Dash me,' said Mac, clutching his head in mock surprise. 'I knew there was something keeping me in check.'

He went over to his wife, who turned her head in pretended disapproval. 'What a welcome!' she exclaimed. 'The poor girl must be wondering what she's got herself into! Look here, my dear, take no notice. He's supposed to be house-trained.'

Mac was already taking her coat as his wife showed Belinda to an armchair on one side of a large open fireplace.

'I'm kinda knocked for six,' admitted Mac, his grey eyes twinkling across at Belinda. 'The last professor we had visiting—well. . . .' he shot a glance at Chuck and made a shape in the air with his hands. 'I guess they come in all shapes and sizes.'

'Now that's enough of that,' reproved Mrs Mac. 'She'll be thinking she's got among a lot of roughnecks, not decent fur-trading folks, as you make out.'

Chuck went to sit on the arm of Belinda's chair. 'So long as I'm around you watch your step, old man,' he said. Then with a grin at Mrs Mac he said, 'I always thought you had him under proper control, but I can see I'm going to have to keep an eye on things out here. You've been left to your own devices for too long.' He patted Belinda's arm. 'Don't worry. Civilisation is just a radio call away.'

'You represent civilisation, do you, lad?' twinkled Mac, taking out one of his pipes and beginning to make it up. 'Gawd help us all.'

'That's fighting talk, mister,' said Chuck from between clenched teeth, and pretended to square up to the older man.

'Boys, boys!' cried Mrs Mac, 'let the poor girl have her tea in peace, coming all this way.' She brought a tray over and set it carefully down on a wooden table beside her guest, then poured everyone a cup of tea.

Belinda noticed that the Eskimo women had come up to the door but had now wandered away.

'We'll go down to the clubhouse later on,' Mrs Mac told her, 'and you can meet the rest of the folks. Things are a little quiet at the moment. But come ship-time, the settlement will fill up again.' The open-hearted warmth of the welcome made the unpleasant little incident on the runway fade from Belinda's mind, and in no time at all she was swapping talk with the Macs.

Mac Macdonald himself had been a fur trader with one of the big companies for almost thirty years and his wife had come out to join him when she was in her early twenties. Two sons and a daughter had been born and the couple's spell in the far north had been broken only by a ten-year stint at the company's headquarters in Toronto while the children finished their schooling. Now that the family had grown up and spread their wings the two had returned to the post they had run in the early years of their marriage, and although Mac was approaching retirement now, it was clear that he would hang on as long as he could turn in a good day's work.

Belinda told them that she didn't expect to be around the post for long as she was hoping to make immediate contact with the Nasaq and if possible travel around with them for a few weeks, until she had got all the information she had been instructed to—as she spoke she was aware of a partly-concealed look of surprise flash between Mac and his wife, and when she stopped talking Mac leaned forward, his cheerful face at once serious.

'Have they told you these people are nomads?' he asked her closely.

'Why yes, of course,' replied Belinda with a shrug, 'I know that.'

Mac sat back, a look of puzzlement on his face. Mrs Mac put in a word.

'It may be difficult to make contact just like that,' she said. 'They don't take kindly to strangers and they rarely come down to the trading post like the rest of the folks around hereabouts.'

'You see,' said Mac, 'it might take a little time for you to get yourself adjusted to life out here. Take it easy, that's my suggestion. See how things pan out. Get to know some of the local customs, make friends with the Eskimos on the post already. They'll be your best source of information. In a few weeks we'll be due for the big freeze-up, then the place really looks like a fur trading station. There'll be people coming and going and then the news really flies.'

He settled down, blowing huge billows of smoke in the air. 'When we first came out here the Eskimo would take his team of dogs and be gone for weeks at a time, following the herds of caribou or hunting deep into the north after seal or polar bear. But things are different now. He doesn't need to run a team of dogs, what with snowmobiles and such like, so he doesn't have to hunt merely in order to fuel his dog team. For that reason he need only be away for short periods of time. He can go after only the choicest furs. He can be much more selective. It means that the old style Eskimo is fast dying out.'

'Yes,' agreed Belinda. 'That's why I'm here. To get on record what they were really like before they disappear completely.'

Mac blew another plume of smoke. 'For all that, though,' he went on, 'things are very different here from anything you've experienced in the big city. Not just language, but customs, travel——'

'If I can just ask a sort of greenhorn question,' Belinda butted in apologetically, 'if they no longer have dog teams, how do they usually travel?'

So far as she had seen from the plane the tundra was

unbroken by roads of any but the roughest kind around the settlements. Vast tracts of the tundra appeared to be totally without the means for conveying transport in any form.

'That's where I come in,' said Chuck, putting down his empty mug. 'You'll have to charter me.' He grinned. 'I hope it won't be too long before you'll be taking me up on that.'

Belinda looked puzzled. 'You mean I have to fly everywhere?' Her mind was aghast at the thought of what it might cost.

Reading her mind, Chuck said, 'It's a good cheap system.'

'But what about when the snow comes?'

'We put on skis,' said Chuck cheerfully. 'Or you can hire a snowmobile. That's a motorised sled,' he added, noticing her look of puzzlement.

'Sounds fun.' She eyed him keenly.

'It is. Remind me to show you how it's done next time I'm up.' He began to put on his jacket. 'I expect I'll see you after the freeze-up if not before.' He moved towards the door and then rather abruptly turned to look at her. He seemed suddenly shy for all his earlier brash good humour. 'Don't get too depressed if you don't manage to make contact with the Nasaq,' he told her. 'There's only one white man they seem to accept around here, and I wouldn't recommend my worst enemy having anything to do with him.'

He shot a glance across the room to where Mac was tamping his pipe. No words were needed. The look of complicity which the two men exchanged was enough to convey Chuck's meaning.

Belinda glanced enquiringly from one to the other. Mrs Mac, alert to the suddenly charged atmosphere, gave a short sigh and started to clear away the empty tea things. Her voice was harder when she spoke. 'Don't worry, young Chuck. We're here to keep an eye on Belinda. Mac will set her right.' Chuck grinned, his boyish face seemed to relax. With a lift of his hand and a last rather obviously telling glance at Belinda, he was out of the door.

The Macs and Belinda went to stand on the front porch. In a moment they heard the aircraft come alive and they watched until he tipped his wings at them and fast became nothing but a speck in the sky.

When they went back inside Belinda turned to her new hosts. She was puzzled. 'What was Chuck trying to say just before he left?' A frown troubled her brow. 'I'm quite capable of looking after myself, you know. I don't know why he said I shouldn't have anything to do with the one white man who seems to know these people. I should think he's just the man I need.'

Mac shifted in his armchair a trifle uncomfortably and began to fiddle around with his pipe as if too busy to answer her all at once. He seemed to take an age to clean it out to his satisfaction, but as he was refilling it with a fresh lot of tobacco he began to talk again, this time, with a grave expression. 'There are some tough customers in these parts,' he began. 'It's the nature of the country, of course. A weakling wouldn't survive a winter in a place like this. You've got to know how to make proper use of the natural resources in order to stay on top. Death is impartial when it comes down to it. Hunting, trapping, they're all simple enough when you know how, but a man needs to be skilled in all sorts of ways if he's going to live outside a trading post as far north as this one of ours.' He looked kindly at her over the top of his reading glasses which for some reason he had put on when he started to talk to her. It was as if he was trying to give her reassurance over something which he found difficult to put into words.

Belinda looked back at him steadily. From what she had seen so far of the country there was nothing to contradict what he was now telling her. She shrugged, not sure where he was leading. 'What sort of man would choose this kind of life?' she asked.

'Ah!' said Mac. 'My very point!' He paused. 'We do well enough on the trading post. Things aren't easy, but we're only a call away from the emergency services. But outside the post——' he gesticulated to the wild grey spaces beyond the settlement. 'Don't get me wrong—I'm not saying that everyone who comes to live in this part of the world is on the run from the law. Of course they're not all fugitives.' She gave him a careful look. 'Some come here because they have a need to prove themselves. Mebbe a lad has a highly developed sense of adventure. He wants to pit himself against the elements and come out fighting. What passes for civilisation nowadays is too soft an option for them.' His wife touched him gently on the shoulder, and for a moment something special seemed to pass between them both. Belinda was moved.

'Yes, I can understand that—the feeling of challenge,' she said quietly. The thought flashed through her mind that perhaps she too, in some small way, had been fired by a similar spirit of adventure when she had agreed to take on Derek's assignment. There was a moment's pause in the warm, smoke-filled room.

'It's a lucky man,' said Mac, breaking the silence, 'who can find a woman who understands.' He changed his position on the sofa and sighed. 'Not everybody comes out here solely for the adventure of it. . . .' He seemed to search for words.

'It's a small community,' broke in Mrs Mac impatiently. 'What Mac is really trying to say is that we know the Eskimos. We know them all by name. We know who's who, and they know us. It's like one big happy family. But sometimes a stranger comes to the area, and he keeps himself to himself. He makes no attempt to get to know anybody. He doesn't let anybody get to know him. Nobody knows where he comes from, why he's here, and he gives no explanation.' She too let her words tail off. She looked closely at Belinda to see if she was getting the drift.

'You mean there may be something such a man doesn't want anyone to know? Something he'd prefer to keep secret?' Belinda sat looking into the fire for a moment or two. When she looked up her eyes were perplexed. 'This is really about the man Chuck mentioned, I suppose?'

'He's a loner,' said Mrs Mac.

'Nothing wrong in that,' broke in her husband. 'But there have been stories. All we can do is warn you.'

'He might have done anything,' added Mrs Mac.

'But surely the Mounted Police patrol the region?' asked Belinda in surprise. 'They would know if a man had a record.'

'They can only check out bona fide suspects. And besides, there's nothing to stop a man changing his name. Look,' said Mac on a new note, 'I'm the last person to go spreading rumours about a man. He's hardworking, brings in some good furs when he needs to trade. Most of the time he's out living native in the Devil's Gate area. He might be able to help you if you can catch up with him. He never stays around here for long. But as Chuck says,' he shrugged, 'I can only advise you to be careful.'

'But if he knows these people I'm supposed to be tracking down, he could take me straight to them, couldn't he?' persisted Belinda.

'They're nomads, they're on the move all the time. Whatever you find out, you're going to have to cover some distance in your search. There are better and trusted native guides on the settlement who would be able to take you wherever you need to go.' Mac settled himself with an air of finality in the sofa. 'You've plenty of other avenues to explore at this stage of the game,' he told her severely, sensing rebellion in her face. 'One thing you'll learn if you stay here long is that everything has its own time. Be patient. If you're meant to meet up with the Nasaq, they'll show. You wait and see.'

Mrs Mac leaned forward. 'It'll be ship-time early next

week,' she told the troubled girl. 'Then you'll get a chance to meet the local tribes who work the northern regions. They'll all come into the settlement to trade. They won't hang around long after the ship leaves. But they always come in for ship-time to trade their deerskins and pick up supplies for the winter.'

'I've already put the word out that there's someone here wanting to meet the Nasaq. It'll get back to them, don't ask me how, and if they're willing to co-operate you'll hear from them one way or another.'

'Perhaps the Nasaq themselves will come too?' asked Belinda tentatively, but her hopes were dashed at once, for Mac shook his head.

'Not a hope, I'm afraid to say. I've told you, they're wary types, keep themselves strictly to themselves. They live well enough in the old way. This is rich caribou country. What do they need with us?'

'I expect one could live quite well off the land,' surmised Belinda. 'There are so many lakes and rivers here it must be simple enough to find food.'

Mac shook his head, smiling. 'That's another greenhorn remark,' he told her, not unkindly. 'Every lake is packed with trout. It's a fisherman's delight. But the Eskimo won't touch them unless they're on the brink of starvation. They eat caribou, caribou and more caribou. Straight uncooked meat.'

Belinda turned her nose up. 'Yes, I remember that. It's where the word Eskimo comes from, isn't it? It's Indian for "eater of raw meat". I can't say I fancy it.'

'It's an acquired taste,' said Mac, his eyes twinkling again. 'We'd have gone bust as a trading station if we'd tried to set up a store, selling, instead of buying. Isn't that so, love?' He turned to his wife. 'If there's caribou they'll touch nothing else. You can see the sense of it when you think that by the time they're beginning to look round for something to supplement their stocks the lake is frozen six feet thick. It's just not worth the effort of breaking up the ice. You'd need a jigger to get through so as to set your nets, and they haven't the patience for that. Though of course they'll sit for hours on the ice above the blow hole of a seal, waiting for it to come up for air.'

Belinda was beginning to yawn. It had been a long day.

'This girl's sleepy,' said Mrs Mac sympathetically. 'Let her come up and have a look at her room. You bring the bags up, will you, Mac?'

He got up without demur. As he did so he shot a glance at her pink jacket hanging on the back of the door.

'You'll have to get something a bit more serviceable than that,' he told her bluntly, and she coloured, remembering the tones of the stranger who had spoken so disparagingly to her when she first arrived.

When the bags had been brought upstairs and Mac had returned to his position on the sofa downstairs, Mrs Mac showed Belinda her room, and the bathroom across the landing. 'Don't be put off by Mac,' she said, turning to the girl. 'He's a bit tactless sometimes. It's a very pretty jacket.'

'Yes, but I suppose I can see what he means,' answered Belinda without rancour. 'It was cold enough coming out in the plane. If I'm going to be travelling overland, I shall certainly need something a little bit more practical.'

'Don't give it a second's thought,' answered the older woman easily. 'I'm sure we can find you something nice in the store. You don't have to stump around looking like the wild man from the north merely in order to keep the frostbite at bay.' She turned to go. 'When the freeze-up comes you'll really know what cold is, and then you'll be glad to go native.'

Belinda sank wearily down on to the freshly made-up bed when the door closed. She was feeling shattered by the sudden changes which had taken place since that morning. It seemed like a lifetime ago. For the first time since taking on this piece of research she was alone with the responsibility. She was determined to make a good job of it. But it looked as if it was going to be trickier than she had at first thought. Carefully she unpacked her tape recorder and notebooks and arrayed them neatly on the little pine table Mrs Mac had provided.

She was ready to drop into bed and let the luxury of a good night's sleep wash over her. But first she lay there with her eyes open listening to the unaccustomed sounds outside and thinking over the day's events. It had been a day filled with kindness from everyone she had met.

The hair on the back of her neck prickled slightly. Perhaps not everyone. There had been that trivial incident on the runway.

She sighed. Silly to let one small encounter spoil the memory of a pleasant day. She turned over and closed her eyes. Tomorrow she would get to know the Eskimos on the settlement, maybe do a little exploring on her own and pick up what information she could about the Nasaq. It was disappointing that she was going to have to wait until news filtered in about her quarry. Perhaps a way round that would present itself.

Again she felt a slight touch of something like fear, and impatiently she changed sides.

By hook or by crook she would persuade someone to take her to where the Nasaq were encamped. She would meet them and make her recordings of their almost lost language. Derek would be glowingly proud of her. They would become friends after all this overheated emotion had burned itself out. She would make her own small contribution to the world of scholarship and everything would be wonderful again. The sorrow of her parents' deaths still hung over her like a pall, but she clenched her fists under the duvet. Nothing was going to stop her winning through.

The last sound she heard as she at last drifted into sleep was the lonely howling of a north wind that had sprung up from across the lake. If she had got up and walked down that way she would have seen the lake covered with white caps and streamers of spume, whipped to an icy froth by the increasing violence of the wind. But she was asleep with her dreams of the morrow.

CHAPTER TWO

BELINDA woke in the early hours of the morning to the sound of torrential rain lashing against the bedroom window. She thought about those people who were living out on the tundra and how they must feel to be listening to such rain and wind without the protection of a proper roof above their heads, and she got to wondering how anybody could willingly choose to live like that. She lay there for some time, drifting between waking and sleeping, until the smell of bacon and eggs and freshly-ground coffee brought her fully awake.

The rain was still beating on the window panes as she washed and dressed, and it gave no sign of letting up. She had a quick look through her clothes and plumped for a pair of smart cord pants, a T-shirt, and a big sloppy blue sweater to top it all. If she had to venture out of doors—and she peeped out between the curtains to stare in amazement at the quagmire on what had been yesterday's landing pad for Chuck's Anson—she could always put on the smart waterproofs she had brought to wear in the city. They were light, but in this, anything was better than nothing. She gave her shoulder-length blonde hair a good brushing. If Mrs Mac's promise to find her some more suitable clothes held good, she would be quite happy to go native in matters of dress. Any kind of serviceable gear would do in this place. It wouldn't matter what she looked like just so long as they kept her warm and dry.

Snapping a band casually round her hair, she went across the polished timber floor to the hall. Mrs Mac greeted her warmly. 'See what you make of that,' she said, placing a plateful of bacon, eggs and tomato in front of her.

'I met the man you mentioned in Toronto,' said Belinda as she ate. 'He's quite an authority on linguistics.'

'I never heard him speak a word of Eskimo all the time he was on the settlement——' Mrs Mac paused, 'though I daresay he knew a lot about the language.'

Belinda looked across at Mrs Mac and they both laughed. 'Oh well,' said the girl, 'I suppose I shall be in the same position. It's far too short a time to get even a basic grasp, but I expect I'll get a chance to pick up the odd word here and there. All I'm expected to do at this stage is collect some recordings of ordinary conversations about everyday things. I hope you'll be able to introduce me to a guide who can also speak some English.'

Mrs Mac nodded. 'No problem there. Just so long as you can be patient. The best man is Taqaq, but Mac won't be able to spare him until after ship-day.'

Half an hour later, having demolished rather more than she expected, Belinda had helped clear the breakfast things and was now standing at the window of the sitting room looking out at the still pouring rain.

Mac, with oilskins over his parka, and wearing heavy-duty sea-boots, had disappeared in the direction of the big store shed, and Belinda had watched several figures go in after him. Obviously some of his regular workers at the settlement were busy in there. He had told her that he employed one man, an Eskimo, on a full-time basis, and the man and his wife and children lived in one of the houses clustered with the others farther up the track. But just before ship-time other families would straggle in from outlying areas and with the men from the families living in the settlement houses, would make up a reliable work force. They had to prepare the big store shed to receive a good six months' supplies when the ship came in, and of course, everything had to be stored systematically so that the more perishable goods could be got out first.

He suggested that if the rain let up a bit she could come round the settlement with him later that morning and meet some of the families living there. One never knew, but someone might just happen to know of the present whereabouts of the Nasaq. There was always somebody with a brother or a distant relative of some kind, a cousin or a seal-partner, who had picked up some piece of news from somewhere. 'They're very sociable people,' he told her with a smile. 'It wouldn't surprise me if the Nasaq already know about you.' Belinda had no chance to ask him what this mysterious expression seal-partner meant, for he was off then, stamping through the puddles across to the store shed.

The rain showed no sign of letting up. It was as persistent as ever. Mrs Mac was busy going through the mail Chuck had brought in with him the previous day and she promised to take Belinda down to show her off to everyone later. Already there seemed to be a scurry of figures heading into the building, and Mrs Mac explained that there was a large room at the end which was used by the natives for communal activities, a sort of clubhouse, much used by the youths in the long winter nights when the freezing weather filled the settlement with people and activity. News of her arrival had already brought quite a crowd into the room and when the hall door opened briefly there was a babble of women's voices and much laughter.

'I don't think we'll wait for Mac,' said Mrs Mac. 'Come down now. We'll make our introductions right away.'

When they went into the room, it was packed with people. Mainly women and children, they sat cross-legged on the floor or squashed up on benches along the wall. Everyone was talking and laughing. The air was steamy as their rain-sodden furs began to dry out in the heat from the stove.

It seemed to be the custom to shake hands with everyone on first meeting, even with the littlest child, and one
by one they filed in front of Belinda, hands outstretched,
tiny tots being lifted up by their mothers.

Belinda felt quite dazed by the end of the session, as
Mrs Mac had told her the name of each person as they
touched hands. Just as these introductions were coming to
an end some of the men from the store came in. Briefly
Belinda's eyes travelled over them—five men, all Eskimo.
She didn't understand the feeling that suddenly swept
over her, as if some expectation had in some way been
crushed. But she didn't have time to dwell on this for long
because the whole process started up again. She must have
met everybody in the settlement that evening.

Much later, during what Mac called 'mug-up time',
Mrs Mac brought up the subject of getting Belinda kitted
out in some rough-weather wear. 'I should let her try
those caribou skins that were brought in last season from
Intuq's lot.'

A look flashed between them. It was something which
did not escape Belinda's notice.

The interior of the store was cool and rather dark, Belinda
found next day when she followed Mac through the big
wooden doors. She threw back the hood of her turquoise
waterproof to get a better look at the place. It seemed to
be a typical general store with a long wooden counter
stretching round two walls, separated from the shelves by
a couple of feet, just enough to allow Mac and one of his
assistants to get by. Everything looked very neat and
orderly, pans and cooking utensils hanging from hooks in
the ceiling, and a variety of tinned and dehydrated provisions arranged on the shelves. Some of the men were
working on the far side, shifting boxes and generally
clearing up.

There was a lot of empty space now and Mac explained
how they would have to estimate their needs months in

advance. Ammunition, traps, all the essentials for the traditional Eskimo way of life were featured, as well as the
more ordinary needs like flour, sugar and tea. 'It's not
exactly up to city supermarket standards, is it?' smiled
Mac, 'but then we don't cater for the casual shopper.
We're a trading post, not a corner shop, and we're only
set up to handle the basics for survival.'

Just then the door opened and a tall, fur-clad figure
came in. He noticed Belinda at once, but he didn't bother
to acknowledge the fact. Instead, he seemed more interested in the quality of some traps over on the opposite
side of the store, and kept his head down busily. Belinda
too turned her back. He was the last person she wanted to
cross swords with at the moment. She felt distinctly uncomfortable.

Mac was speaking to the men and Belinda heard one of
them say 'Nasaq', after which there was a general shaking
of heads. The effect on the newcomer was startling,
though. His head jerked up, then he shot a strange look
at Belinda. When she caught his glance he raised an eyebrow sardonically. Blushing furiously, she turned away
and pretended to be inspecting some of the furs on one of
the shelves. At that point Mac came back to her. 'No
luck, I'm afraid,' he told her in English. 'They seem to
have gone to ground somewhere north of Hell's Gate.
Nobody seems to know much.'

Belinda tried to turn the conversation at once to the
question of which furs she could try. That man was un-
ashamedly listening to everything Mac was saying. How
dared he eavesdrop on a private conversation? thought
Belinda in a fury, what confounded cheek! And so blatant
too! Now he was moving over to the men. As he approached Belinda could not help noticing how they all
fell silent and one or two stepped back slightly as if getting
ready for something. Out of the corner of her eye she saw
him talking to them, fast and fluently, but even if she had
been able to hear what he said, she wouldn't have been

able to understand it. The men shook their heads again, and one of them looked over to where Belinda and Mac were standing. Abruptly she turned to the furs and selecting one at random held it up for Mac's approval.

'Too small,' said Mac at once. 'Here, let me find you something.'

While he was rummaging through the jackets the white man came over. 'Put this on the account, will you?' He showed Mac some lines he'd picked out. No 'please' or anything like that, thought Belinda. Apparently he had the same high-handed attitude to everyone, the boss of the trading post included. He was unshaven and a dark stubble covered his chin. 'That's a mighty pretty fur,' he drawled in a mock-Canadian accent, with a strange, ironic glint in his eye as he levelled his glance at Belinda. She lifted her chin and didn't answer. The man made no move to leave. Mac had nodded his assent already to the man's request, and there was a slight pause. Belinda fumed inwardly. How could she choose a decent jacket with this arrogant man eyeing her in that suggestive manner? Or was it just imagination? Was he simply pretending, playing some sort of game with her, as if that was the approach he thought she wanted?

She raised her eyes coldly to meet his glance. 'I'm not frantically interested in pretty furs, actually,' she said, and even to her own ears her voice sounded prim and prissy. She went on: 'I'm much more interested in getting something practical and plain.' There was a wealth of meaning in the word plain, as if to say, rough and dirty and workaday too. She added, with a smile: 'Something like your own working clothes, perhaps.' Her mouth curved sweetly when she turned away. 'What do you say, Mac? Something plain and practical? I'm not too concerned with my appearance at the moment.'

Not put out at all, the man made an ironic mock bow, and as Mac went behind a pile of sled equipment, he said out of the corner of his mouth in a perfect English accent,

'I'm sure the lady will look fetching in anything—or nothing at all.' He smiled, clicked his heels, and turned to go.

Belinda was speechless with rage. The man's attitude was beyond all limits! He was a perfect stranger. How dared he? They had both been partially obscured by the equipment hanging from the ceiling and Mac had not overheard anything. It's not worth making a fuss, thought Belinda. They did warn me against him last night. By now he was at the store room door. She watched as the door closed behind him, then one of the Eskimos came over to them. He said something to Mac. Mac looked briefly concerned, then turned to Belinda with an apologetic shrug.

'News about the Nasaq,' he told her, unable to keep the note of apology out of his voice. 'It could just be they've gone on a seal-hunt up north.'

He paused, and Belinda got the feeling that he was unsure how to break a particular piece of news to her. He stroked his grizzled beard for a moment.

'Be gone for some months if so. Might not even come down hereabouts at all this year.' He shot her a cautious sideways look as if to gauge how she was taking this bit of bad news.

Belinda sighed. She turned away, digging her hands deep in the pockets of her jacket. For a moment there was nothing she could say. When she turned back to the two men her eyes were bright with the steely glint of determination. 'How sure is this information?' she asked.

'Rumour. Only rumour,' replied Mac quickly. 'Bear it in mind so you don't build up your hopes too high. But wait on till ship-day. There'll be something definite then—one way or the other.' He turned to the man who had come up to them and put an arm on his shoulder. 'Here's your guide, anyway—Taqaq. Speaks English.'

As if to prove it, the young Eskimo said: 'Hello.' Belinda gave him a warm smile. This was one of the men she had met the previous day in the clubhouse. She hadn't realised he spoke English.

'What do you think, Taqaq? Do you think the Nasaq are going to appear?'

Taqaq gave a brilliant show of teeth as he smiled, but nevertheless his prediction was gloomy. He spread his hands helplessly. 'We shall wait and see. It would be no picnic to track them into the far north.' His eyes fleetingly took in the slim body of the girl in front of him. 'Very tough country. My people work lines only a hundred miles from here, but that's far enough north for me.'

'Don't like the cold, do you, Taqaq?' Mac laughed, and Taqaq joined in.

'That's why I'm here,' he laughed. 'Nice and warm, no?'

Belinda raised her eyes in mock horror. 'If this is warm . . .!'

'You've seen nothing yet,' rejoined Mac. 'Come on, let's have another look for something that'll keep you snug when the freeze finally does come.'

Taqaq wandered off to his duties at the other end of the store with an assurance to Belinda that news wouldn't be long in coming through, and she and Mac delved into the pile of furs once again for something suitable.

In no time at all they had come up with something in the right size, and Belinda donned it with curiosity. She certainly had had no intention of striving for effect, but somehow the light-coloured furs brought out the blonde of her hair and gave her skin a creamy, delicate look. She felt a little silence fall on the men as she came forward to look at herself in the full-length pier glass, and Mac nodded in appreciation. 'If I was twenty years younger,' he quipped. 'I'd show these young 'uns a thing or two!' He turned to his men, then looked back at Belinda. 'You'd better not come down here very often. I'll never get a scrap of work out of them. Come on, lads,' he shouted jovially, 'you'll have your wives after you!'

The men grinned and carried on reluctantly with what they were doing, and Belinda glanced in the mirror again. She felt like a million dollars. The natural sheen of the fur seemed to set off the glowing translucency of her complexion, and she caught Mac giving her another appraising look.

'Come on,' he said, 'get yourself off to show Mrs Mac before I go making a fool of myself.' He put an arm protectively round her shoulder and ushered her towards the door.

The rain had all but stopped by now and at last the relentless drumming on the wooden roof was beginning to slow down, making conversation easier. Together they sloshed back across the compound to the house.

Some time later, after being duly admired by Mrs Mac, Belinda was looking out of the window wondering whether the rain which had now stopped altogether was going to hold off long enough for her to take an exploratory walk down by the lake. As everyone seemed to be busy she eventually went along to her room to get her pink jacket. It was far too warm, comparatively speaking, to go out clad from top to toe in furs, and despite the criticism her jacket had brought from Mac she was truly pleased she had brought it with her. In a few moments she was walking briskly in the direction of the water.

The foreshore seemed at first to be completely deserted. It was only when she approached the water's edge and turned back to look at the land that she noticed a figure working on an upturned canoe on the beach at the far end of the inlet. As her footsteps were already leading her in that direction she continued to walk slowly along the edge of the lake, glad at last for a breath of fresh air and the peace and quiet afforded by the lakeside scene. It was a harsh landscape, however, and there was a threat in the ominous grey sky which, though brighter, was still unbroken by any gap in the clouds. The lake itself seemed dark and forbidding as she sauntered along its edge, and when she got a little farther along the beach towards the solitary figure working there she resolved to stop and exchange a word of greeting. She was only a few hundred yards from the settlement, but already she could feel the desolation of those barren miles stretching without a single inhabitant to the Arctic Circle.

Belinda quickened her pace, a call of greeting rising to her lips, but it froze suddenly without being uttered. The man had raised his head and now turned towards her. It wasn't an Eskimo after all. It was the white man again— the tall, tough, sardonic trapper who regarded blondes as commodities and whose presence in the store shed earlier that morning had seemed to cause such a stir. She hesitated. She would look silly now if she turned back. The man would think he had some sort of power over her. On the other hand, she didn't want him to think she was making overtures, as if she was a woman desperate for the company of a man, any man, no matter how arrogant and insulting, or—she quivered—or how dangerous.

A flicker of apprehension rose up as she remembered Mac's warning. It was a lonely spot. She hesitated, unsure what to do. Then the decision was abruptly taken from her by the man suddenly coming towards her. In a few long strides he was across the shingle and standing, tall and erect, in front of her. She refused to back away, although every instinct told her to turn tail and run. She felt dwarfed and threatened by his proximity. He was certainly a tough-looking customer in his deerskins and with his dark hair coming almost down to his collar. Now that she could see his face clearly she noticed the deep mahogany tan of his skin. It was relatively unlined, making him younger than she had at first supposed, but there were deep lines in the corners of his eyes as if he had spent much time looking into the sun, or across the white dazzle of the barren snows. His eyes, of a frighteningly cold blue, swept her body arrogantly, and she felt her skin flush beneath her hood as if he had stripped her naked.

Her lips were set in a tight line. He needn't think he was going to get anywhere with her! Just because he was the only white man for miles around. He had another think coming if he thought she was the type to start running after every man in sight! She half turned as if to go. As yet he hadn't spoken; his eyes had been too busy looking her over. Belinda's blood boiled. She half turned back, some tart phrase springing to her lips, but before she could speak his lips had formed the hint of a smile and he said sneeringly: 'So what have we here? A lady sociologist?' He gave a short laugh.

'I'm surprised you know the word,' she retorted sharply, 'and anyway, you're wrong. I'm a linguist.' She glared at him. But instead of being abashed by her reaction he started to chuckle.

'Even better,' he said. He was now openly laughing. 'I suppose you don't even speak a word of the lingo and have to do all your talking to the natives through an interpreter?' His eyes sparkled with malice.

Belinda clenched her fists. 'A linguist doesn't necessarily have to speak every language they research,' she told him cuttingly with as much dignity as she could muster. 'We make comparative studies of different language groups. If you knew the slightest thing about it you'd know that.' Her eyes blazed.

He shrugged his broad muscular shoulders as if it was all the same to him. 'You must be crazy, a woman alone, coming out here.'

A shiver ran up and down Belinda's spine, but she raised her chin. 'Actually, I quite like it. Everyone's so wonderfully kind. There are exceptions, of course.' She gave him a dark look, but it made no impression on him.

He ignored her tone in such an infuriating manner that Belinda's blood was seething again. He went on talking as if her reaction was simply of no consequence whatever.

He would bat away the irritations of a mosquito with exactly the same level of indifference, she thought irritably. She was too angry to catch all that he was telling her. It was something about a professor from a college down south. Yes, she probably knew who it was.

'A self-styled expert on the Eskimo,' he was saying. 'Read a lot of books about them, and that was all. Then he came out here as a linguist—going around with his little notebook. No one ever heard him speak a word of the language the whole time he was here. Some of the natives had a high old time, as you can imagine!' He focussed his startling blue eyes on her, daring her to join in the joke. Belinda averted her glance.

'Yes, I suppose you would think that was funny,' she said disdainfully. 'Wasting people's time and money.'

'Time and money? That's serious!' He mocked her with his eyes.

'Yes, it is!' she interrupted, her voice beginning to rise. 'Don't you realise, if it wasn't for people like him the Eskimo language would die out? It would be gone for ever. No one would ever know it had even existed. It's like—it's like——' she searched her mind for some example that would make him understand—'it's like the caribou—if they died out, no one would ever know about caribou.'

'And you think that's important?' he asked with amusement.

'Of course it's important!' she exploded. 'It's our duty to conserve everything precious and beautiful and unique.'

'And you think the Eskimo language is all those things?' he asked.

'Don't you?' she riposted angrily.

'Not really,' he said. 'It's not all that beautiful as languages go. It depends on what you're used to. I'm not interested in that sort of thing. Beauty leaves me cold.' His glance roved her body insolently, then his face became serious. 'What is important is how functional something is. Does it do its job? That's what concerns me.' He paused. 'If fewer and fewer people see the need to speak a certain language,' he went on patronisingly, 'that language gradually falls into disuse, so what?' He shrugged. 'If a thing is no longer useful, discard it. Junk it. Throw it away.' He paused again. 'So-called civilised man keeps too much. Cities are becoming nothing but living museums. You city folk exist in the past, among dead things, among useless memories. Cities are nothing but graveyards of old ideas.'

'But it's history, it's civilisation.' she expostulated. 'It's what we are. It's our heritage. The past shapes us.'

'We are what we are at this moment. Not what we were ten, twenty years ago.' His face grew suddenly tight and a shuttered look came over his eyes.

'What do you know about civilisation anyway?' said Belinda scathingly. 'Living here, with only the bare elements for a decent standard of living? It's not as if you're even attached to the trading post with a proper job——' she stopped.

'So they've been talking about me, have they?' His eyes looked cold and the sneer came back into his voice. 'The civilised white folk clustered together in their little cabins as the wolves howl outside in the night——' He stopped abruptly. 'Mac's a good man within his limits. He's fulfilling a useful function. It's civilisation that's gone soft—civilisation, with its urge to collect and collate every living, breathing thing. You academics are nothing but carrion. If something is on the verge of death, there you are flocking round the corpse with your little notebooks, and your column inches of copy.'

'That's journalists. Column inches—we don't have to write in column inches,' she broke in sarcastically. 'It seems you've chosen the appropriate habitat for yourself, miles from anywhere, no chance of meeting up with any of the people you seem to despise so much. I suppose you can feel safely superior to the natives. While they're forced to scrape a bare subsistence from the land you can come along and play at Eskimos. You're like some Victorian white hunter, pretending to go native. You know you can always go back to civilisation.'

'Can I?' he cut in sharply.

Belinda stopped, in confusion, but her anger with him rose up again, placing the words in her mouth. 'I suppose you can only see yourself as a Mr Big when you're among pygmies.'

She turned away with a toss of her head.

'Pygmies live in Equatorial Africa,' he remarked drily to her retreating back. 'Perhaps you need geography as well as language lessons.'

The words stung her, but she refused to turn back and she didn't slow her pace till she had marched all the way up the beach to the track leading back to the settlement.

Even then her face was flushed, her heart was pounding and her thoughts were hammering angrily in her head. Of all the confounded arrogance! The sheer unadulterated cheek of the man! Just because he hadn't approved of one researcher there was no need to damn the lot of them! She was furious. Graveyards of ideas? Carrion? But it was his lazy scrutiny of her body that had really rattled her. It wouldn't surprise me if he already had a couple of native wives, she told herself. These men usually finish up like that. Coming out here for heaven knows what reason. Fugitives from justice, Mac had said. Then going native, but keeping just so much distance between them so that they could play the big white chief and take what they wanted with impunity. How on earth could he expect her to swallow all that stuff about civilisation? she asked herself. He must think she was some naïve young girl straight out of college. Couldn't he tell she had worked for a full year since graduating? She was no ingénue when it came to life. She couldn't be bamboozled by such poppycock. She knew what was valuable about civilisation and what wasn't. She had standards. He was nothing but a drop-out!

She stamped about furiously outside the kitchen door before going inside as if she was shaking the last of the rain from her boots. When she opened the door she was still flushed and Mrs Mac looked up from her baking in surprise. 'That was quick,' she remarked. 'Had a good walk?'

'Fine,' replied Belinda shortly.

'Mac tells me you've had no luck so far.'

'What?' Belinda looked at Mrs Mac for a moment. 'Oh, no,' she replied, collecting herself. That man had momentarily put all thoughts of the Nasaq right out of her mind. 'I expect we'll hear something soon, though.' Mrs Mac prinked the edge of her pie expertly and started to dust the top of the pastry with flour. 'You can always ask Barron. As Mac said, if the worst comes to the worst, you can but ask his advice. He spends most of his time up there in that region. He's almost one of them. I hear he's still around the camp.' She shot a glance in Belinda's direction. 'I'm surprised you haven't bumped into him yet.'

Belinda was taking her boots off by the door. She scarcely raised her head, her thoughts were still in angry turmoil. 'Who's Barron?' she asked without interest. 'That doesn't sound like an Eskimo name——' her words trailed off. She looked open-mouthed at Mrs Mac, but now she had her back to Belinda and was busily adjusting the shelf inside the oven. She turned briskly back.

'That's right,' she said as she carefully placed the pie on its rack. 'It's not Eskimo because he's not Eskimo. I thought Chuck told you about him yesterday?'

'You all warned me about someone,' replied Belinda, stressing the word with a grimace.

'You know why Chuck was so concerned,' said Mrs Mac. 'I don't think there's any mystery about that.' She laughed. 'Chuck's a nice boy, but faced with a maverick like Barron, sparks are bound to fly. Chuck does a tough job, flying that aircraft in all weathers. He needs to settle down with some nice girl. He's certainly not short of female companions,' she continued, giving a sideways look at Belinda, 'but he hasn't met that special someone yet.'

A little frown began to furrow Belinda's brow. She came over to the kitchen table, perfectly at ease in the assured hospitality of Mrs Mac, and began to munch one of the apple cores left over from the baking. The frown did not leave her face, but it wasn't the daredevil Chuck she was thinking about. She munched thoughtfully for a few minutes. At last she said, 'This Barron or whatever he's called——' she paused; she knew she was clutching at straws, but it had to be asked, 'apart from you and Mac is he the only other white on the station?' She waited expectantly for Mrs Mac's reply.

'There are one or two Eskimos who speak enough English to be able to act as guide. I was only thinking he might have some information they haven't got,' answered Mrs Mac infuriatingly.

Belinda sighed. 'No, you don't understand. I mean, if I'd happened to meet another white man on the station, it would be this——' she shrugged, not wanting to say the name again.

'Barron?' put in Mrs Mac helpfully. 'Yes, I should think so. Unless some trapper had come staggering in from lord knows where.' Mrs Mac smiled. 'That's not very likely, though. We're five hundred miles from the nearest trading post and nobody's gone out from here recently.'

Belinda sighed again. Her worst fears were confirmed. Not only was the disreputable Mr Barron again said to be the most likely source of help, he was also emphatically the last person she was ever going to go to, cap in hand, begging favours of any sort. Not when she knew what he thought of her and her colleagues. Not when she had had to suffer yet again the indignity of those lazy blue eyes exploring her body so insolently.

She sighed again. The man was dangerous too, Mac had said as much. She had every reason to keep away.

She made up her mind to be patient. She would do as they had advised her last night. Everything had its own time. Eventually the Eskimo would bring the news she wanted.

All she had to do was wait till ship-time. She could do quite well without the help of Mr Clever Boots Barron. She would be patience itself.

CHAPTER THREE

IN the days that followed Belinda found it difficult to cultivate the frame of mind she had decided upon. Her natural quickness and desire to see results was difficult to bring under control, and every new arrival into the settlement was eagerly quizzed, by means of an interpreter, as to the whereabouts of the Nasaq.

Sometimes Mac, sometimes the smiling Taqaq, would act as go-between, but so far both of them had drawn a blank.

Belinda had to admit that after a certain person's criticism, she felt a bit of a fool having to rely on someone else in order to have even a half-way decent conversation with anyone. Her helplessness in this respect made her feel childlike and at the same time deeply irritated with herself. As a result she secretly started to pick up as much basic vocabulary as she could—secretly because she knew it was a crazy idea even to hope to learn more than a smattering of the language in the short time she was to be in the region, and also because she did not want anyone to think that she was just another jumped-up academic, arrogantly assuming that she could casually pick up suf-

ficient of this intricate language for her own purposes, only
to drop it all when she returned to the outside world.

It was lucky that she had a natural flair for languages.
Sometimes it seemed that she could just pick words out of
the air. Slowly, but surely, she made some progress.
Fortunately Mrs Mac was very busy and left her to her
own devices once she had established that Belinda was
doing essential 'desk work'—and it was through many
painstaking and rather lonely hours that she began to
make sense of the unfamiliar grammatical structures of
the local speech.

'Don't spend too much time poring over your books
and things,' remonstrated Mrs Mac one evening as
Belinda started to make her excuses after dinner.
'You ought to take a rest now and then. Though I don't
know——' she paused, worriedly, 'there isn't a great
deal here for a girl your age.' Her kindly eyes took in
Belinda's tired face and drooping shoulders. 'It's a pity
there aren't any companions for you.'

Belinda's thoughts involuntarily strayed to the someone
she was resolved never to think of again. Companion was
hardly the appropriate word anyway for that sardonic
antagonist. She forced the thought back savagely. Neither
hide nor hair had been seen of him since that day down
by the lake. And a good thing too, she thought with
venom. At least no one else had told her she was carrion.
Everyone was kindness itself.

She brought her thoughts back to the present. 'If you
think I'm spending too much time alone,' she said, 'I'll
take a stroll along to the club-room.'

'Yes,' brightened Mrs Mac. 'Even if you can't say much
they can practise their English on you.' She heaved a sigh
of relief. It was more of a responsibility than she liked to
admit, putting up a young career woman like Belinda.
Although she was very fond of the girl, they really had
very little in common. Why a pretty girl like Belinda
should want to bother herself with a career when she could

be married with a couple of bonny children was past Mrs Mac's understanding.

By the time Mac came through to the club-room on his rounds before bedtime, there had been a good hour and a half of lively laughter and rapid quick-fire conversation in two languages. 'I'm teaching English,' Belinda told him as he came through the door. 'They're very quick.' She was surrounded by a group of children.

'They're cheeky enough in their own language,' he replied, ruffling the hair of the nearest youngster, 'without giving them extra ammunition.'

'Well,' yawned Belinda, 'I think I've had enough for one evening. There'll be new arrivals tomorrow, they say. Maybe we'll hear something about you-know-who.' She had already written to Derek, describing her flight and reception here, and she had thought it worth mentioning that there were already difficulties in establishing contact with his wandering folk. She thought it was as well to warn him so that it wouldn't come as too much of a shock if she did eventually fail in her quest. She pushed the disagreeable thought aside. She wouldn't fail. She would pull out all the stops. Indeed, she felt reasonably cheered by her evening's exertions. Come ship-time there would surely be some news, they had told her, and no one had actually said it was impossible to meet the Nasaq, merely that it required patience. Well, patience was something she had well in hand.

A few days later she was abruptly snatched from her slumbers by a strange commotion going on outside her window. Unaccustomed shouts and running footsteps, the bark of dogs, strange in itself when so many of the Eskimo used motorised transport, and a deep and distant hooting from the direction of the lake like some sort of foghorn assaulted her ears. No sooner had she opened her eyes than she was out of bed and scrambling into some serviceable clothes. Time for a quick splash of cold water on her face and a hurried brushing of teeth and she was across the hall and into the kitchen at full pelt.

'Is this it?' she called to Mrs Mac as she pulled on her parka. 'It is, isn't it? It's the ship!' A glance out of the window showed that it was true. Out in the lake, riding at anchor, was the supply ship.

'Anybody would think you'd been starving for the last six weeks and were desperate for food supplies!' chided Mrs Mac to the retreating girl. 'Don't forget your coffee!'

Belinda had got Mrs Mac's over-generous breakfasts down to a couple of slices of toast and honey and several cups of black coffee. Not enough on which to drive a team of huskies, as she remarked to Mrs Mac, but then it wasn't very likely that she would be doing that just yet! Mrs Mac put the coffee pot back on the hob and went over to the door. Belinda had already reached the shore.

It seemed as if everyone had been up for hours. There was already a pile of crates heaped up on the beach, and the outboard motorboat conveying supplies from the main ship was busily chugging back with another load when Belinda arrived.

She sauntered down to the water's edge, unsure how to fit into the scheme. Everything seemed smoothly organised with a chain of people throwing stores from hand to hand all the way up from the boat to the store shed. But she was soon left in no doubt as to her role when one of the women threw a small sack with signs that she was to follow to the store with it. Laughing, Belinda joined in. Soon she was part of a team which seemed to include everyone from the settlement. Even the smallest child seemed eager to take its part and a line of children trooped dutifully up and down the beach, adding another element to the happy almost party-like atmosphere that was beginning to develop. They worked steadily all morning.

Mug-up was brief as everyone seemed eager to get as much equipment into store before nightfall. They were soon busy tramping back and forth again. Belinda

watched as countless times the outboard chugged to and
fro between the ship riding at anchor in the lake and the
now well-trampled beach path. It was perhaps on the
fifth or sixth time after mug-up when the boat turned and
headed out, riding high and light in the water, that her
glance, casually sweeping the shoreline, fell on a dark
figure moving steadily away towards a bluff of rock at the
far end of the inlet.

There was only one person it could be. Only one, she
thought, who was too stiff-necked and arrogant to join in
with his neighbours. A real loner, she thought, anti-social
in the extreme. What chain of events had brought such a
man to this lonely place, a place made even more desolate
surely by his resolute refusal to muck in with communal
activities? How did he spend his days? How could he bear
the solitude with no one to talk to from one day's end to
another? She felt a surge of compassion which she quickly
brushed aside. It was pointless shedding sympathy on a
man who so patently did not want it. He had made it
quite clear that he thought himself superior to any other
living being.

Especially blonde lady linguists from England.

She realised she still smarted from the patronising tone
in which he had said 'lady sociologist', as if she was some
kind of dilettante, playing at academic research, whiling
away her own time and wasting everybody else's in some
pointless game. She would jolly well show him what she
thought of that view!

She lugged another load up the beach. It was only when
she reached the bustle of the store shed with Mac standing
calmly and in control amidst the apparent chaos that she
allowed herself to frame the thought that had been
troubling her all morning. She had become swept up in
the air of anticipation and excitement that had been
building up in the settlement as ship-day approached,
with the result that she had somehow managed to shelve
her anxiety about meeting the Nasaq. With every day

bringing new arrivals it had seemed inevitable that sooner or later, as everyone had reassured her, someone would be able to tell her where the tribe were now hunting. But it was now, when ship day had arrived at last, that she began to feel a resurgence of her earlier anxieties, and she was beginning to have serious qualms about her adopted method of waiting so patiently for news. It had brought no result. And today, with the ship anchored out in the bay, and the last of the most distantly domiciled trappers having straggled in late last night, it looked as if her hopes of hearing something useful were to be dashed.

She couldn't let Derek down, she simply couldn't. Nor could she let herself down now. The frown deepened.

'What's up, love?' asked Mac, at once noticing her troubled face as he came inside. He paused for a moment in his tallying. 'If it's too much for you, you're free to go and sit down. Nobody expects you to work like this——' he looked with concern into her clear blue eyes.

'It's not that,' she sighed, brushing a stray lock of blonde hair from her forehead. 'It's just that——' she haltingly explained her anxieties to him. For once he offered no consoling reassurances. Busy man that he was, he made as if to put down his tally book.

'No, it's all right,' she said, noticing the movement, 'we can talk later.'

With a slight look of relief Mac put another carbon between the pages. 'We'll be finished by nightfall,' he told her. 'We'll have a chat this evening.' As she started to turn he suddenly stopped her. 'On a lighter matter,' he said, 'I'd like you to do something for me.'

'Of course,' replied Belinda. 'What is it?'

Mac smiled. 'I forgot this last time and they sailed away with the lot,' he grinned. 'Just a few personal supplies,' he told her. 'I want you to go out in the boat next time and call in at the Captain's cabin. He's got one or two things for me under lock and key, and I want you to pick them up for me. Sign the bill of lading and check that everything tallies. There's a case of Scotch and one of rum—for Christmas,' he added with a grin. His eyes twinkled. 'It'll be a dry do if we let that damned skipper sail away with it again!'

Half an hour later she was on board the supply ship and could look back at the shore where the scurrying figures were making short work of what remained of the previous load.

Idly she noticed that young Ikluk, previously absent, was now walking along the beach towards the busy group. The girl started to lift a large box, but another woman came up and a short argument seemed to follow.

Ikluk seemed to turn away, then she put the box down and went over to a pile of small bags. She picked several of them up and joined the others on the path to the stores.

Belinda forgot the girl almost straightaway.

Christmas! It was strange to think of Christmas in this place. A land of snow and ice, it should be appropriate somehow. She herself would already be far away in England, bracing herself against a cold that was nothing compared to what these people would be enduring.

How could they stand this endless cold? she puzzled. It would have to be something very strong that could keep her here for more than a few months. Imagine giving up all the benefits of central heating, and bright, clean, modern housing to live in a wooden shack, or worse, a corrugated custom-built unit like the ones beginning to spring up even as far north as this. Imagine not being able to go out to the cinema whenever one felt like it, she thought, pulling a face. Nothing, but nothing, could make her want to stay out here for good.

Her gaze briefly roved the length of the beach. It was visible from end to end from this position out in the bay, but it looked as barren and desolate as the hills beyond it—apart from the orderly chaos on the landing dock. Belinda was angry with herself for letting her thoughts continually skirt dangerous ground.

He must find something to keep him here, she speculated. Something. Or perhaps someone. She chided herself for allowing any space in her thoughts for such a man.

It's as if there's a sort of vacuum in my mind which he seems to fill up, she mused, climbing down into the pitching boat. In normal circumstances I wouldn't attach any importance to such a trivial encounter. But somehow— somehow it seems to have acquired such mind-bending importance. She sighed. I suppose it's because I'm having to spend such a lot of time alone. I'm just lonely, that's what it is. A little tear of self-pity formed in the corner of her eye. If there was somebody other than the Macs to talk to—if Chuck and some of his friends could be here more often. She jutted her chin. She would not give way to tears like this. For a moment she longed to be back at home, to see Derek's grey eyes holding her own with the half ironic, half caressing gleam of old. How she longed to be back in the junior staff common room, bandying words with her colleagues over some tiny point of logic. She shook herself. Heavens, she was only here for three months! It wasn't forever. What was a little solitariness in all that time?

By the time the boat's prow was gouging up the sand and the man with the painter was leaping ashore to drag the heavily-laden boat farther up the beach, she was momentarily restored to her former eager anticipation of events. It was certainly true that there was plenty to take her mind off things this morning. No time for tears. Once the day was over there would be time for taking stock and making a realistic assessment of her progress so far in furthering Derek's project.

With a mournful farewell call on its foghorn the ship was starting to pull away. Belinda went to the window and watched as the lights slowly faded. The departing ship was soon out of sight. Ship-time was over for another year.

'Well,' said Mac genially over a glass of hot rum as he sampled his Christmas package later that evening, 'what shall we do about that little matter that was bothering you earlier today?'

'I don't suppose any news has come through, has it?' she asked tentatively. Her eyes looked up soberly to meet his. She both hoped and feared what his answer would be.

Apologetically he spread his hands. 'If I didn't know these people better,' he said thoughtfully, 'I'd almost suspect a conspiracy. It's very unusual for nobody to know the whereabouts of a tribe like them.'

'Talking about the Nasaq?' asked Mrs Mac. Her husband nodded. He looked across at her, his eyes clouding briefly before he spoke. 'There was a story that they'd gone out to the ice fields after seal,' he said at last. Then he shrugged.

'Who told you that?' asked Mrs Mac.

Her husband paused tellingly. 'Barron,' he said. 'At least, that's what he told Taqaq.' He sighed deeply. 'There's something not quite right about it.'

Before she could reply there was a commotion at the outer door and it flew open to reveal a figure in glistening furs. The man shook himself like some huge healthy animal before shooting a cold-eyed glance round the room. Belinda felt her face heat up as his blue eyes seemed to bore through her before he spoke.

'A word with you, Mac?' he said, turning his head abruptly.

'Well timed,' said Mac, indicating the newly opened bottle on the table.

'No, thanks,' replied Barron curtly. He sat himself in an empty chair on the other side of the table as if reluctant to join the intimate little group round the fireside.

Standoffish as usual, thought Belinda, her hackles rising. I suppose he thinks he's too good for us. She half turned away and took a sip from her glass. 'This is very nice, Mac,' she said, turning her eyes on him in a smile that effectively cancelled out Barron's boorishness.

Mac acknowledged her with a tilt of his glass. Turning to the newcomer, he said, coldly this time, 'Well, what can I do you for?'

By this time Barron had got up and was taking off his outer boots. He seemed to take a long time to get them off and when he finally came soft-footed back to his chair Mac had started to fiddle around with his pipe as usual. Belinda carefully avoided even the smallest glance in Barron's direction once he sat down and she waited for the two men to speak.

'Well?' asked Mac, eventually breaking the silence.

'Did you see Ikluk?' asked Barron, ignoring Belinda altogether.

'Yes. Still no news?' Mac nodded in Belinda's direction.

The girl held her breath. There was a short silence. Unable to bear it for long, she finally gave in and said: 'News about the Nasaq?'

Barron's eyes avoided hers. He shrugged his broad shoulders in a sign of boredom. 'There was a story that they'd gone out to the ice fields after seal,' he told Mac, as if it was no concern of Belinda's.

'Who told you that?' broke in Mrs Mac, impatience leading her to join in the conversation at last.

'One of the men.'

'That doesn't sound quite right,' mused Mac half to himself.

'Are you trying to say I'm lying?' Barron raised his dangerously sparkling eyes to gaze long and silently at the older man. Despite his quiet tones there was an edge to his voice which seemed to make the old fur trader draw back in his chair and grip its edge.

Belinda felt a stillness fall over the little group and she became suddenly conscious of the distance stretching away outside the wooden building, the desolate, inhospitable wastes where a person could call for help in vain. She noticed with a sudden shock the proximity of Mac's gun on the wall by the door, and the knife, no toy, its hilt heavily bound, protruding from Barron's thick leather belt. With all her senses alert for danger she said quietly, 'Why should they go out to the ice fields at this time?' She felt Barron stir slightly as if becoming aware of her presence, but the danger in the atmosphere seemed to ebb as quickly as it had come, with the sound of her voice.

Barron gave a short laugh. 'Seal, of course,' he replied, his eyes momentarily piercing her steadfast glance with a look like a small stab wound. She recoiled from his sharpness and dropped her gaze. Fighting a rising tightness in her throat, she took a firm hold on herself and slowly, very slowly, raised her eyes to his. 'Why is it nobody seems to know anything for sure? You say "there's a story" as if it has no real foundation in fact. Someone, surely, must know something?'

Barron didn't reply at once. As if to break some spell of inactivity which had settled on them all, Mrs Mac got up to busy herself in the kitchen, and just then there was a rattle from the radio in the next room and Mac too got up.

'That's my call coming in for Paulatuk, by the sound of it. I'll have to leave you.'

Suddenly alone with Barron in the intimacy of the fire-side glow, Belinda became acutely conscious of his narrowed blue eyes levelling on her. She licked her suddenly dry lips. 'How far away are the seal grounds?' she forced herself to ask.

He shrugged nonchalantly without letting his glance leave her face. 'Far enough,' was the reply.

'Surely there must be some way of tracking these people

down?' She waited for some response, but the mocking gleam in his eyes told her nothing. 'I suppose I shall have to charter a small plane,' she went on.

'Have you the money?' His glance became narrowed with surprise. Now it was her turn to shrug noncommittally. She didn't see why she had to tell him all the details of her project as he had so far shown such marked lack of interest. She raised her chin. It was no concern of his that Derek had let her know that if unexpected expenses arose she should use her own discretion. She was fully aware that there was a ceiling on what she spent and she had no idea how much it would cost to charter a light aircraft, but Chuck would be able to advise her there. She set herself against asking Barron any further questions. Let him do the asking if he was so inclined. Unless he came up with some positive sign that he would help her, he could ask till he was blue in the face, she was answering nothing.

For a long moment there was unbroken silence, then slowly he turned his head as if bored with the whole business. 'Have you any idea of the vast area you would have to cover? The thousands upon thousands of square miles of tundra and pack ice?' he asked. 'There's no sure indication of where they are, just a vague hint that they might have gone north.' He waved his arm to include a ninety-degree angle, and Belinda had a shuddering vision of the vast desert wastes beyond the lighted settlement. Barron settled back with an air of finality as he spoke. 'Anyone can see you're wasting your time. Your damn fool professor should have given the matter some proper thought instead of sending you out on a wild goose chase like this. But then that's the academic world for you—no idea when it comes to practicalities.' He gave an infuriating grin, and added, 'At least you have a chance to get out before the big freeze comes. Those winter winds would play havoc with your hair.'

For a brief moment Belinda felt like hitting him. She

seemed to hear a voice telling her to hold her tongue, but her blazing anger quenched any sign of caution, and she felt her fists bunch and her eyes shoot daggers at him as she told him in no uncertain terms precisely what she thought of him. 'Who do you think you are anyway?' she asked hotly. 'How dare you criticise a man like Derek? You haven't even met him. He's extremely well thought of in circles where academic excellence and personal integrity count for something.' Barron's lips compressed themselves into a hard line at this, but she went on regardless. 'He warned me exactly what I was taking on. What's more, he knows I'm not going to fail—because I'm not! So you can think again if you imagine I'm just going to turn tail and go home like a meek little girl on your say-so!'

She realised that she was beginning to sound prissy again, that for some reason he seemed to bring out the schoolmarm in her with his insulting remarks about her hair. It was as if he thought she was just an empty-headed young girl who could be easily put in her place. I'll jolly well show him, she told herself fiercely, gritting her teeth. His gibes about her seriousness really rankled.

'I must say you've been extremely unfortunate in the kind of women you've met up till now if you really think a little bad weather will send me scurrying back to England!' With a toss of her head she made as if to get up to go, but with alarming speed his hand shot out and pinned her back into her chair. Before she could object he was speaking in a hard, angry voice.

'Listen,' he hissed, 'it's a dead duck, this jaunt of yours. Forget it. All you'll be doing is making extra work for the rescue services. It's a hard country, no place for a white woman, you just haven't got what it takes. If you've an iota of common sense you'll get right back to where you belong.'

Vainly wriggling to free herself, Belinda raised a face to him scarlet with anger. 'Just get your hands off me!' she breathed. 'Do you want Mac to come in and find you behaving like a barbarian?'

'Mac?' scoffed Barron, his handsome face breaking into a brief, devilish grin. 'And what's old Mac going to do? Throw me out?'

He released her and stood up to his full height. He had a magnificent physique—enough to deter any man from mixing in with him.

Belinda glowered from her place in the chair. 'You're so tough,' she sneered, 'you only dare lay a finger on me because you know you can get away with it at the moment. If I wasn't alone you wouldn't dare come within a mile of doing such a thing.'

'If you weren't alone you could no doubt be persuaded to act sensibly,' he riposted. 'Any man would realise by taking one look outside that this is no time of year to be holidaying.'

Again the scorn in his voice and the choice of words brought flames of angry colour to Belinda's cheeks. Fearing to raise her voice in case Mac came running through, she answered him in a voice of repressed savagery. 'I've heard about as much from you as I want to hear,' she told him. 'Now just get out and keep your nose out of my affairs! I'll handle this my own way.'

As soon as the words were out she realised she had overstepped the mark. An angry glitter came into his mocking eyes and he stepped close up to the chair and gripped her tightly by both shoulders.

'Did you tell me to get out?' he whispered close to her face. She was acutely aware of his lips almost brushing her cheek. She tried to wriggle away, but he held her in such a tight grip with her head flung back against the cushion that she was unable to move.

'No one has ever, ever told me to get out,' he whispered again. 'I certainly don't intend that a jumped-up little schoolgirl should start.'

Her heart was beating furiously, but she managed to

croak out a few words of protest.

'You can't be allowed to get away with that,' he went on, pulling her hair a little to still her wildly moving head. 'You'll be getting ideas above your position.'

'You're just feudal!' she managed to say. 'I'm as good as you any day!'

'Is that a challenge?' he asked humorously. 'I'd like to see you last two hours out in the wilds when winter really comes.'

'You're pathetic!' she spat. 'And you're a bully. I hate you!'

Barron's eyes gleamed and Belinda was about to cry out as he tightened his grip on her when there was the sound of Mac coming through from the radio room. At once Barron straightened up, releasing her with a little push that sent her farther back against the chair, but when Mac came walking through, it seemed as if the two had merely been having a quiet conversation by the fireside. He came over to them, already reaching out for the bottle, and again offering Barron a drink.

Barron thrust his hands nonchalantly into his jacket pockets and said something about having to get back. He gave a sardonic glance at the flushed-faced Belinda.

'I've told Belinda all I know. I think we've exhausted that rather fruitless topic for the moment. What I really came to see you about, Mac, was those new traplines you were going to have sent in.'

The two men moved to the farther side of the room while Belinda, finding it difficult to conceal her fury, poked the logs in the fire and made the sparks fly. I'll show him! she told herself furiously. He'll have to eat his words. No man gets away with that. How dare he treat me with such contempt!

A few minutes later the men had finished their conversation and Barron was busy putting on his boots by the door. When he was ready to go out he gave a long, slow look in Belinda's direction. She had just raised her head and her glance was held for an instant before she turned away with an angry toss of her head.

He came over to where she sat and seemed to tower over her. There was a challenging look in his eyes when he spoke. 'If you're still waiting for the plane back to Paulatuk by the time I get back here in two or three days' time, come and see me. You never know, there may be something of interest I can tell you.' His eyes mocked hers.

'I doubt that very much,' she replied coolly, 'unless you have definite news about the Nasaq.' She looked coldly up at him. 'I doubt whether there's anything else whatsoever you could tell me that would hold the slightest interest for me.' She got up suddenly and for a moment they stood body to body before she turned abruptly away, confused by the rush of feeling that such proximity brought in its wake.

In a few moments he was gone. Belinda ran agitated fingers through her hair. 'Well, Mac,' she said, trying to calm the shakiness in her voice, 'what do you think of that? Do you think the Nasaq have really gone to ground?'

'The whole thing sounds fishy to me,' muttered Mac thoughtfully. 'There's a very effective jungle telegraph out on the tundra. It's nothing for a group to be out hunting—they'll stop, set up a rough camp, have a mug-up, spread the word to other groups, they like to gossip, and there's always someone meeting up somewhere. News is passed on more rapidly than you'd ever imagine.'

'It seems strange,' chimed in Mrs Mac, 'nobody knowing anything.' She looked across at her husband.

Belinda leaned forward, her face tinged with a warm glow that came not only from the radiance of the stove. 'It seems there's only one thing for it——' she paused and took a deep breath, then she stopped. Suddenly Chuck's words came back to her—'There's only one man they seem to accept . . .' and she remembered how he'd paused and how his tanned young face had hardened momentarily, and how the warning, which he had tried to make as casual as possible, had made Mac and Mrs Mac exchange glances in evident embarrassment. True, they knew nothing specific against the man. Now Belinda was finding it difficult to use his name even in the privacy of her thoughts. He filled her with such distaste. She felt that where no specific accusation was made, room was left for all kinds of speculation. Perhaps he *was* simply a renegade, a man who despised society so much that he cast himself out of society rather than the other way around, or perhaps he had fled to this remote region for reasons of a personal nature—disappointment in love, a broken marriage.

Belinda snorted inwardly. Such a man had no tinge of gentleness in his make-up. It was impossible to imagine him touched by any hint or sign of compassion for another human being, let alone imagine him giving himself up to the love of a woman. His hard mouth, the chipped ice of those blue eyes that sent disagreeable shudders up and down Belinda's spine were enough to show that love or anything like it was foreign to his nature. Barron was like a dangerous animal, unpredictable, mysterious, with motives and manners far removed from the norm. The way he had spoken to her, articulate, obviously well educated and intelligent, made him more than some simple son of honest toil, trying to wrest a living with his bare hands from the inhospitable lands of the North, and the very fact that he was so cultured gave an added smell of danger to the man. It lent him the aura of a wolf, clever, subtle and unpredictable.

Fear momentarily made a coward of Belinda. She let her words tail off into silence. Surely, she argued with herself, it was common sense to think that if none of the natives knew of the whereabouts of the Nasaq this man, a foreigner like herself, would be unlikely to have access to any special information? Just because he had set himself up as some sort of guru, living outside the small community here, it didn't mean he was any better, despite what he seemed to think of himself.

She was falling for the same line as everyone else, regarding him with a special kind of frightened awe. Witness the men in the store the other day, the way they had kept their distance from him. True, he was physically big, a tough, hard-muscled man, and must seem almost like a giant to these small-limbed people, and that in itself must have given him a certain standing in the community. But that was no reason for Chuck, a muscular young boy in peak physical condition, to have a similar attitude of awe towards the man. She sighed. Was his attitude due to fear or merely, as Mrs Mac had hinted, to a boy's sexual jealousy when a girl he was sweet on seemed destined to cross the path of another potential suitor? She thrust the thought aside as too fanciful. Her contact with Chuck had been brief, no more than a meshing of looks. Yet she knew it could be more if she so wished. It was nonsensical if Chuck actually believed such a man could hold any sort of romantic interest for a woman like herself. Without undue humility she knew she was an attractive woman, that her background was such that she could hold her own with anyone. It was surely taking fantasy too far to suspect that Chuck would even give a passing thought to the possibility of her and—— Again she hesitated over the name. How could he dream of such a thing! As if a girl like her would look twice at a rough-hewn backwoodsman like—— As if she would so lower her sights to include a man who, for all his fancy talk about civilisation, lived in the most primitive conditions imaginable. She? Indignation darkened her eyes for a moment. Only when she pictured Chuck's worried face did they soften. Of course it was nonsense to think that he had seriously considered the idea of her becoming attracted to such a ruffian.

It was surely concern for her safety which had prompted his dark warning. Instinctively he saw the threat of vio-

lence in the man, saw his lack of respect for the conven-
tions of civilised behaviour. He would feel particularly
helpless, flying around the country in a light aircraft, with
no chance of developing a relationship properly. Poor
Chuck. Her lips softened into a curve. He had no reason
to fear for her on that score.

She leaned back and rested her head on the soft cushioned arm of the sofa. Her thoughts were once again in
turmoil. When Chuck had issued his tentative warning
Mac and Mrs Mac had immediately agreed with what he
said. They had accepted Chuck's request that they should
look after Belinda as if there was something perfectly
reasonable about protecting her from the outcast. As if
the danger from him was real.

Belinda eased the muscles at the back of her neck. She
felt tired and tense, and not only from the day's unaccustomed activities.

She remained with Mac and Mrs Mac until bedtime.
The crackling log fire slowly subsided amidst glowing
embers, the fiery caverns of light in its depths glowed and
faded, and Belinda's thoughts, finding no solution to her
questions, themselves gradually slowed and faded into a
gently dreamlike state. Only when she felt her eyes involuntarily closing did she make an effort to shake herself
awake.

Mrs Mac gave a soft laugh. 'You've been overdoing
things, young woman,' she said gently.

'It's that or the rum toddy,' laughed Belinda, shaking
herself awake. 'It's so nice here I could sit in front of the
fire all night.' She yawned and stretched.

'No solution, then?' asked Mac, knocking out his pipe
and beginning to put it away for the night.

Belinda yawned again. The strange, dreamy inner
compulsion that had taken hold of her earlier was as
strong as ever. No amount of rationalisation seemed to
affect it. It was simply that now she felt no desire to talk
about her plans. The decision, whatever the outcome, had

been made, and further talk was unnecessary. She stood up to go. 'There is only one solution,' she told him, repeating her own words from earlier in the evening. She smiled down at her host and hostess. 'I'll just have to sleep on it.' With that, she bade them both goodnight and went up to bed.

CHAPTER FOUR

As casually as possible, Belinda walked down the track leading to the beach. Now that the supply ship was no longer out in the bay the shore of the lake was again deserted. Focus of attention today was on the store shed and there had been a constant coming and going between the houses and tents of the settlement and the big wooden warehouse which now stored the means for survival through the approaching winter months. It seemed as if every family group was busily engaged in preparations for the big freeze, and Belinda had inevitably found herself watching with fascinated admiration as the trappers had crowded round the stores, selecting and testing the new equipment with a seriousness and expert intentness which was in stark contrast to the mood of jollity which had prevailed during the previous day's task of unloading the same equipment. As everyone was now so busily engaged, no one noticed her slip away after lunch, and she reached the water's edge without exchanging a greeting.

Ever since the previous day the weather had taken a definite turn for the worse, and Belinda slipped into her new deerskin parka with a sense of relief. It was the first time she had had an opportunity to wear it since the day she had shown it to Mrs Mac, and when she felt the first icy blast of wind from off the lake on her face she was more than pleased that she had been persuaded to discard the pink quilted jacket for something no less attractive but certainly far more practical. She had taken Mac's advice in the foot department too, and sported a pair of sealskin boots over soft leather moccasins. In this gear she now stood hesitantly by the leaden lake. Her heart was beginning to beat over-rate at the thought of what she was about to do. Silly, she chided herself, anyone would think this was an interview for a new job, instead of a simple visit with a simple request. The man could only say no. She drew a breath, then turned her face resolutely towards the bluff of rock that thrust itself jaggedly into the sluggish waters of the inlet. She didn't know the exact location of his abode, nor even whether he was still around, but she had seen him several times walking either towards or away from the rocks, so she guessed he must live somewhere in that direction. If not, surely the unusual height of the bluff would give her an adequate view over the surrounding low-lying terrain.

She set off doggedly, head bowed against the biting wind which blew along the length of the inlet. Anything was better than sitting in the house waiting for news which didn't come, she told herself, and by the time she had reached the foot of the rocks, she had talked herself into a high feeling of expectation.

It was only a short climb to the top, but a sigh of disappointment escaped her when she saw nothing but the unending emptiness of the plain beyond. There was a track of sorts and, with eyes fixed intently on the faint markings on the ground before her, she set off to follow where it led. It was several minutes before she reached the scattering of stunted trees which had seemed to represent such a danger when she had been sitting white-lipped in Chuck's noisy little Anson. Now the constant moaning of the wind through the branches seemed to accentuate the desolate silence which surrounded her. With a vicious little tug of fear she remembered that wolves and even bears were known to roam the region.

Surely the chances of their coming down so near to human habitation was remote in the extreme. Or was it? With the freeze approaching what could a greenhorn such as herself know about the habits of the local wildlife? Her assignment was a purely academic one. Such details when contemplated from the safety of her study had seemed irrelevant. She gave a shaky little laugh. This wouldn't do at all. Where was the girl who had told Derek to leave it all in her hands? Here she was now, shaking like a leaf simply because the wind moaned in that eerie way.

She set off at a run through the trees, and, breathless, came out on the other side in a wide shallow valley. Her eyes widened. She had certainly found her man. Or at least, she had found his lair.

Mouth open, she gazed incredulously at the little shack in front of her. The same familiar shape of the winter snow-houses, it was a simple frame structure covered with skins. Belinda paused for a moment, not sure whether to call out or what. Still goggling that anyone could actually live in such a primitive place, she started to make her way over the lichen-covered rocks. For some reason she felt a strange, prickling sensation running down the back of her neck. It made her stop abruptly. Then, almost without realising it, she began to turn slowly round to face the way she had just come. With a flicker of panic she saw, standing there on the path behind her, silent and unmoving, the man Barron. Fighting an irrational fear, she realised that her escape was barred. He must have followed her all the way through the wood. She shivered when she realised that he must have seen her stop in fright at the sound of the wind, and he must have been laughing to himself when he saw her hesitate outside his shack. He was laughing now—or at least, his lips were drawn back to reveal dangerously sharp white teeth, but his eyes glittered with an ambiguousness that could have owed more to malice than to humour.

Belinda's throat went dry. She tried to speak, but no

words would come. Cursing herself, she thrust her hands deep into her jacket pockets and regarded Barron with frightened eyes. His glance caught and held her own. Slowly, not letting her drop her glance, he began to walk down the path towards her. All Mac's warnings came flooding back to her. There was no escape. She stood her ground, but as he got closer she could feel her lungs bursting with held breath and the nails of her fingers cut into her palms. He came to within a few yards of where she stood. Not knowing whether he was going to strike her or—she let out her breath, gulping in air, poised ready for fight or flight. Once again she felt overwhelmed by the sheer physical presence of the man, by the primitive savagery of his face, by the startling icy blue eyes, which were now fixed unwaveringly upon hers as if to draw the very soul from her body. A barely perceptible groan escaped her lips and she felt powerless to move. For what seemed a long time, neither of them spoke. Then, in a voice of surprising quietness he said: 'Forgive me. I'm not used to visitors.' He moved slowly away in the direction of his shack. 'It's not the Ritz,' he smiled ironically over his shoulder, 'but it is home. Come and have some tea.' It was a sort of command.

Belinda found herself obeying instantly. Only a yard or two down the path, though, she stopped with a little gesture of her hand. He sensed this at once and turned back. He had an expression on his face which she found hard to read. It was watchful and cautious, like that of a hunter waiting to see which way an animal will spring, so much in tune with his captive's mind that every impulse is reflected there in the hunter's face. Belinda tried to take a hold on her flying thoughts. She couldn't explain the feeling of being drawn into something dangerous. There was no visible coercion, nothing tangible to make her feel this overwhelming sense of being in the man's power. Yet when she feebly tried to turn back she knew it was only a vain gesture of defiance.

'I haven't much time,' she demurred. 'I have to get back to the settlement.'

His lip curled in a smile. 'Of course, I forgot. You're busy making notes about the tribe you haven't met. That must be quite a task. You obviously have talent.'

Stung, Belinda opened her mouth to reply, then checked herself. It was no good getting on the wrong side of the man at this point. Despite his strange compelling power, the sneering manner, she was determined to play it cool, to get what she wanted. She shrugged and turned back, her eyes lowering demurely to the ground in front of him.

'I knew it wasn't going to be a picnic when I came out here.' She lifted her clear blue eyes to his, and a shudder went through her body as their eyes locked. A steely glint of battle showed briefly in the sapphire depths and Belinda put up a hand as if to brush back a curl of blonde hair, averting her glance once again.

Abruptly the man turned to his house. 'You've time for a mug-up. Don't go bringing your urban manners here. Time means something in the Arctic. Life isn't a series of deadlines.'

He pulled aside the skin which covered the doorway and Belinda felt herself drawing nearer to where he stood. He moved back as she approached and though she felt only the slightest touch as his arm brushed against her cheek, she felt her body recoil as if stung. He let the door flap down behind them and it seemed as though they were both suddenly and intimately more alone together than was possible even in the desolate outdoors.

Belinda tried to move away from him, to lessen the strange sensation such proximity aroused in her. Her eyes darted about the place, observant and anxiously alert. The house was lighter than she had expected, there being an opening near the roof from which an extra skin had been tied back to let in some light. But it was cramped inside, with only just enough room to stand upright. There was what she took to be a sleeping platform, about twenty inches high, which filled up almost half the floor space. It was covered thickly with skins, and when Barron told her abruptly to sit, she placed herself gingerly on the edge of the luxuriously cushioned platform.

In one corner of it was a bright sleeping bag like the ones used by mountaineers, but apart from that one concession to the world Belinda knew, everything else was defiantly native.

At one side, neatly arrayed, were some pots and pans, a small stove and a stone lamp like the ones she had seen at the settlement. Mac had said they used seal blubber and had been in use by the Eskimos for centuries.

Barron was now lighting the stove and was balancing an already filled enamel kettle on it. His movements were relaxed and easy, like a man thoroughly at one with his habitat. Once again Belinda was struck by the sheer muscular strength of the man. Even in his fur parka she could see the broad vigour of his shoulders, the slow supple movements of his limbs as he went about his task. He came to sit on the platform a few feet away from her while the kettle came to the boil. She wanted to blurt out her request, to get it over with at once, but something in the quizzical glance he gave her made her realise that she should bide her time until the mood was ripe. There was something different about the sense of timing here, she mused, a sense of leisurely acceptance that everything had its own pace, and she remembered that even Mac and Mrs Mac, even though they had a busy trading post to run, rarely used clock time in their conversation. She had heard Mac talking about a journey he had made up to a lake, saying it was only four sleeps away in good weather.

She looked hesitantly into Barron's face. He was smiling inwardly as if laughing at her again. Something seemed to stir deep in the icy depths of his eyes. It was a dangerous spark which made her suddenly conscious of the folly of stepping into his lair, and memories of their previous encounter came flooding back.

He's like a fox or a wolf, she thought, playing with his victim. She checked herself again. She must try to be level-headed. It must be the strange isolation of her situation which was flooding her mind with such disturbing thoughts.

Now he was staring intently at her parka as she looked up and caught his glance. She involuntarily glanced down to see what was wrong. Perhaps he was surprised to find that she had discarded the pink quilted affair so soon. That was one in the eye for him, if he thought she was just an empty-headed fashion-plate. She fiddled with the long fringing on the cuff, wishing he would say something.

Fortunately the kettle came to the boil and, still without exchanging a word with her, he rose lazily to his feet and filled two mugs with the golden brown liquid. Shakily she gulped the steaming brew, eyes darting anywhere but in his direction. It seemed he was adept at playing a waiting game. With a determined uptilt of her chin Belinda cradled the mug of tea and gazed steadily across at him. A suitable space of time had surely elapsed, she decided at last. It was now or never.

After a brief attempt at polite nothings which drew no more than the most laconic yes and no from her host, she put down her mug and turned to face him squarely.

'Last time we met you said you might have something to tell me. I know it's rather soon——' she began.

'Still no news,' he told her positively.

'Then I suppose I'm really here to ask your help,' she went on.

He gave a short laugh.

'I didn't expect this to be a social call,' he replied. 'I can tell you now, the answer's no.'

'But you don't know what I'm going to ask,' she protested.

'No?' he regarded her quizzically again, the hard gleam

coming into his eyes. His lips curved into a malicious smile and he leaned back lazily among the furs. 'It doesn't take a shaman to divine your purpose.' He watched her carefully. For a moment Belinda didn't know whether to speak or wait for him to go on. But he continued with: 'You want me to take you to the Nasaq—wherever they are. You want me to run them to ground for you—as well as no doubt carting all your expensive recording equipment across the tundra just so you can pry into the lives of people who've had the good sense to make themselves as inaccessible as possible to people like you. Well, the answer's no. They're my friends, and I don't inflict your sort on my friends.' He paused.

Belinda took a sip of the still steaming tea. All her hopes had come crashing down. But even worse was the rage which had risen in her at the injustice in his words. Her blood boiled. What right had he to make her feel like this? What did he know of her that he could speak so disparagingly of her? She took a firm grip on the tea mug, so that her knuckles showed white. She would not let him make her lose her temper. Her breath came jaggedly at first, but she fought to bring it under control. When at last she spoke her voice was calm.

'I think you must have some sort of second sight to guess why I came to see you.' She paused, hoping he would be disarmed by the flattery in her voice. 'But——' she paused again and tried to sneak a look at his expression. He was watching her intently. She averted her glance at once and tried to lean casually against the piles of furs. She sighed as if hopelessly and allowed her tongue to caress her upper lip. 'I'm not interested in prying into anyone's life.' She gave him a slow look from beneath her lashes. 'Not anyone's, whoever they are. What people do is their own business.' She hoped he got her meaning. She was fighting to control her anger, but there was no sign of this in her voice.

She turned towards him fully. 'I don't want to change

or hunt down the Nasaq. I simply need to record their language. My professor in England chose me out of several other candidates in the department, and I would hate to let him down. It's a sort of personal debt I owe him.' She looked up at him slowly from under her lashes again. 'Only you can help me, so everyone says.' She paused for effect, then let her voice drop intimately and added, 'I'd be so grateful.'

For a moment there was a silence. Barron's face was impassive and she had no idea what he was going to do. When he leant across so that his face was within a few inches of her own she was totally unprepared for the harsh look of suppressed rage which filled his eyes and compressed his lips into a cruel line. One hand shot out and he grabbed hold of her wrist with a vicelike strength that made her cry out, but unheeding he dragged her towards him. Before she had time to protest he was pulling her to her feet with an angry snarl. 'Get out!' he snapped hoarsely. 'Get out now while you've got the chance. Do you think I'm some sort of fool, that you can come here and try those tricks on me? What do you take me for? Is it so important to you that you'll debase yourself like this for your career? Who is this man in England who can send a girl like you to this sort of place?' He shook her, both hands holding her tightly by the upper arms so that she was powerless to move. 'What sort of woman are you? Do you think I'm so desperate for a white woman that I would betray my friends for . . .' He stopped with an exclamation of disgust.

In horror Belinda realised what he had thought. He had mistaken a little gentle flirtation for an offer of her body. Her heart plunged sickeningly. He still gripped her tightly as she began wildly to protest her innocence, and at the same time she tried to struggle desperately to free herself. 'I didn't mean that,' she cried. 'How could you think such a thing!'

'No?' he looked at her in derision. 'It was a promise,

was it? A promise you would fail to keep after you'd got what you wanted? That's exactly what I'd have expected.' He flung her from him with an expression of disgust.

Belinda lay where she had fallen for a moment, tears of anger and hurt humiliation springing to her eyes. She glared up at him. 'Do you seriously think I would offer myself in return for a favour from you?' she spat. 'Maybe that's the sort of woman you're used to. Well, count me out! I wouldn't touch you if you were the last man on earth!'

She rose shakily to her feet. The bruising of her wrists gave an added dimension to her scorn. 'You?' She looked him insolently up and down. 'Every girl's dream. God's gift!' Her voice rose in a peal of laughter. 'You've lived in the backwoods too long, my friend. Styles have changed. The look of the roughneck desperado isn't popular any more. Most women of my acquaintance prefer something a little more elegant, a little cleaner, a little less redolent of honest sweat and toil, perhaps.' She smiled calmly into his face. Her words had wiped it of all expression. 'The squalid and the primitive has only a limited appeal, I'm afraid. Civilisation has much to offer, and I welcome it all.' Her eyes shone as icily as his own. 'In my world women work on equal terms with men. We don't have a to barter our bodies for a little help. There are enough people around with sufficient generosity of spirit to give help without any expectation of gain.' She let her gaze sweep insultingly round his home. 'You do have delusions of grandeur, my friend. What you can offer a woman seems to me to be precisely nothing.' With a toss of her head she turned to the door.

All this time he had been staring at her without saying a word. His eyes showed no expression, but a pallor seemed to have spread over his face. Suddenly she felt mean. It was like kicking a man when he was down, she thought. His hovel was ample proof of his poverty. But given the circumstances of his situation she had to admit that her jibe about cleanliness was unfounded. Poor though his possessions were, everything shone with the gleam of the well cared for, and the only smell was the natural tang of fur and leather. But it was too late to backtrack on what she had said now. She turned with as much dignity as she could muster and moved the few paces to the exit.

As she reached out to pull back the flap she turned to look at him. He was still standing absolutely motionless near the sleeping platform as if her words had turned him to stone. Not a muscle moved. He seemed coiled within himself. His eyes stared at her without any flicker of interest or feeling.

To her surprise he let her go with no attempt to add or to change what had happened between them, as if he accepted that as the final word between them, so that all the way back to the copse Belinda's thoughts were triumphantly running over what she had told him. Obviously a few home truths were enough to make him go speechless. It must be a shock for anyone to speak to him like that. He had had things his own way too long, playing the big man around the settlement, setting himself apart as if his standards were the only ones worth having. Her triumph gave way to anger when she recalled the feeling of contempt in his eyes when he had looked down at her as she crouched on the floor where he had flung her, and her anger with him gave way to anger with herself when she realised what a dreadful mess she had made of her request.

In view of their previous encounters it seemed only to be expected that this would be the inevitable outcome of any further meeting. She had half expected it to end badly. That was why she had gone overboard in her attempt to flatter and cajole Barron into helping her. Given what she had known of him already, perhaps it had been a silly approach. On the other hand, it was easy to be wise after the event. Belinda was a girl who, if she had set her mind to it, could have twisted any man round her little finger, but she had always preferred independence, not wanting to be beholden to any man, until Derek. By then she had been so weak and confused, she had clung to him out of pain rather than in any calculating way, in order to get anything from him. Now she was strong and independent again, and despised the use of feminine wiles to obtain things which she could get quite simply by shifting for herself.

Resolutely she marched into the shadow of the trees. Already the daylight was fading quickly and it would soon be dark. She would damn well show Barron she could do without his help! She'd get on to Taqaq right away, and they would set out with provisions in the direction of the place where the Nasaq were last seen. Someone somewhere would surely be able to give them a clue.

At that moment she became aware of a small figure hurrying along the path towards her, and as it came closer she realised it was the girl Ikluk. She was struggling along with a bundle of furs in her arms, intent on the path, her eyes downcast beneath the fur hood. As the two girls drew level Belinda waited for the girl to look up. A word of greeting was already on her lips, but to her surprise the girl merely glanced briefly in her direction, her eyes dull with some look of unfathomable indifference, and with no sound, was off down the path towards Barron's house.

'Huh!' thought Belinda. 'So much for the friendly Eskimo. I'm glad they're not all so taciturn.' She felt piqued by the girl's unfriendliness and turned back to watch her hurrying out beyond the trees.

The girl had not altered her speed at all, and a sudden thought jumped into Belinda's mind. With a puzzled frown she watched as the girl reached the edge of the wood and started to make out across the lichen-covered ground towards the hut. Almost without thinking Belinda moved casually into the shadow of a tree and watched as Ikluk approached the hut. She was almost there when she called out loudly, 'Amaruq! Amaruq!' At once the door flap was lifted. She seemed to pause for a moment, then Barron came out. He stood outside for a moment while the girl said something to him, then he took the bundle she was carrying and went back inside. The girl followed and the flap dropped down behind her.

Intrigued by this, Belinda waited a moment. She had no intention of spying, heaven knew. Why should she spy on such a man? What Barron did was his own concern. But she felt powerfully intrigued to think that he had some personal contact with people from the settlement. She remembered the sudden lowering of voices as he had approached a group gossiping outside the store shed, and the nature of his relationship with Ikluk began to interest her mightily. Was the girl perhaps selling him already treated furs for the approaching freeze? But why, if he was the trapper he was supposed to be? Why else should she bring furs to him? What sort of transaction was now taking place inside the hut? Belinda held herself in readiness for the girl's appearance, prepared to carry on up the path back to the settlement the moment she came out, but the door flap remained resolutely shut.

Impatient to be off, Belinda turned, but suddenly checking, she looked back once again towards the hut. What if she walked casually by? Would she hear the murmur of voices from within? Undoubtedly Barron spoke such fluent Eskimo that there would be no point in the girl trying to practise her English. Perhaps he gave informal language lessons to those who wanted them? Perhaps he was trying to perfect his own grasp of the regional dialect? What else from a man like him, so trenchantly determined to go native? He was native in dress, in choice of home, in speech . . . Belinda's blood froze. He lived the Arctic life so thoroughly, as she had seen, this man, with a man's needs—and now the girl, calling out so familiarly—Belinda felt as if the ground had opened at her feet. Suddenly she had to get away. She found herself running, half stumbling, only vaguely conscious of the direction in which she was plunging, driven along by the urgency of her desire to escape. 'Amaruq'—the word beat inside her head like a hammer. What did it mean? What had the girl been calling?

Breathless, Belinda came at last to a halt on the track leading along the edge of the lake. She forced herself to walk slowly, struggling to regain her breath, collecting her teeming thoughts, trying to calm the chaos of her emotions. Her wrists still smarted from where Barron had held her and she knew her hair had become dishevelled by her mad rush through the wood. Pausing for a moment by the grey lake's edge, she tried to tidy herself up, to bring some calm and reason to her mind. When she felt sufficiently composed she started to wend her way back to the house. Even though it was early afternoon, daylight was rapidly fading and the glow of gas lamps shone out softly from the stores. Careful to avoid meeting anyone, she made her way quickly up to her room and closed her door. 'Amaruq,' she repeated, sitting down on the edge of her bed.

She lay back on the blue check quilt. 'Amaruq!' Now she thought about it she remembered hearing a similar word some days previously in the clubhouse. But what had been the context for that particular word? She wrinkled her brow, forcing herself to think hard. It had been when Taqaq had been telling her about a polar bear hunt. Slowly it began to come back to her. 'Nanuq,' he had said, 'polar bear,' and when she had asked the names of other beasts he had reeled four or five of them off so quickly she had scarcely had time to jot them down.

Now she sat up with a feeling that was something like relief. She was sure that was it. She went over to her worktable and began to search through the bits of card

and scraps of old envelope on which she daily listed new
vocabulary. She scanned them rapidly, dropping them
any old how on to the bed until she found the card she
wanted. Yes, here it was. *Tuktu*—she squinted at her
scribbled jottings—*tuktu* meant caribou. And here was
another—*siksik*, ground squirrel—*pangniq*, bull caribou,
amaruq—she paused, an ironic smile curved her lips—quite
what she had expected, what could be more appropriate?
The girl had called Barron Amaruq—'*amaruq*,' meaning
'wolf'. Belinda let the card slip from her fingers. Her
breath came out in a long sigh of something like relief,
but she would have been reluctant to admit that that was
what it was.

She sat on the edge of the bed with the scattered cards
around her. She was remembering something else Taqaq
had said to her. When a boy child was named, he said, it
was the custom to take two little bones from the foot of a
wolf, pierce and string them together, and tie them to the
clothing. That would give the boy when he grew up staying power on the hunt. He would be as persistent as the
wolf in hunting. Well, Amaruq, Barron, whatever he
called himself, had accused her of hunting his friends
down.

She tossed her head. There would be two wolves, then.
If that was how he saw her, let it be true. She would hunt
them down.

He wouldn't be the only wolf around. She herself would
be like the wolf, she would show how persistent she
could be. With an ironic little smile she squared her
shoulders.

The battle was on!

CHAPTER FIVE

THE weather report was coming in over the short wave transmitter Mac had had set up in a corner of the living room. The voice from the weather station crackled and burred, piling information on information, and the old-timer wrinkled his brow and gave a sigh. He looked across at the two women by the fire with a bemused smile. Mrs Mac was busy as ever, knitting needles clicking rapidly as she strove to finish Mac's annual winter woolly. It was an institution on the settlement, Belinda had gathered, and every year, regular as clockwork, a sweater for Mac would appear. Last year it had been a dun, striped affair, he was wearing it today, but this year it was cherry red.

Mac had held the half-finished garment up. 'No chance of getting lost in this,' he had teased, and Mrs Mac had smiled benignly.

'Foiled again,' she twinkled, shooting a smile at Belinda. 'It looks as if I'm stuck with the same old model for another winter!' Now she paused in her rapid work, however, and looked across to where Mac was fiddling with the knobs of the transmitter. She caught his glance. 'Good news about the weather,' she said.

Mac shrugged. 'I suppose those bods know what they're talking about.' He glanced out of the window. 'I'm half inclined to go along with Nuallataq, though. I've never known him be wrong yet.'

'What does he say?' asked Mrs Mac.

'He says it'll be soon. At least he doesn't actually say anything, he just goes quietly and deliberately about his preparations for the freeze.' Mac turned to Belinda. 'In all the years I've known him he's started his preparations at exactly the same time before the ice moves down. It's uncanny. I don't know how he does it. Must have some sixth sense.'

'He's that very old man with the limp, isn't he?' asked Belinda.

Mac nodded. 'In the old days they'd kill off their aged parents, but even in the old days I think Nuallataq would have survived. He's a sort of walking store of knowledge for the rest of them. His disability came about due to an argument with a polar bear as a young man, but it seems to have worked to his advantage. It's given him a sort of sensitivity to nature that comes close to the supernatural sometimes.' Mac laughed. 'He's a bit of an old charlatan. The Eskimos used to set great store by the so-called powers of the shamans.'

Belinda looked up quickly. That was the second time she had heard that word in twenty-four hours. 'Shaman?' she repeated.

'Witch-doctor—a mix between faith-healer, prophet and conjuror. Nuallataq's the local man. He'll tell your fortune if you want him to. He's said to be something of an expert with the divining bones.'

'You scoff,' broke in Mrs Mac reprovingly, 'but there's more than just faith-healing involved. He has an amazing ability with herbal cures. He makes our official first aid box look a bit useless.'

'Yes, give him his due, he cured that stomach upset of mine last spring.' Mac came over to the mantelpiece and selected one of the pipes there. Thoughtfully he began to fill it with pungent tobacco. Belinda watched him for a moment.

'What do you mean when you say they'd have killed him off in the old days?' she finally asked with a shiver.

'Just that,' replied Mac, settling himself on the sofa and putting his feet up. 'They're a tough bunch and life was hard—still is for some. The Arctic is the sort of place that doesn't give a man a second chance. When it's a question

of survival it's necessary to act in a way that would seem
barbaric to our way of thinking. But then we're not faced
with snow and ice and blizzard and the possibility of
seeing our families starving to death. It became a question
of honour among the oldsters. As soon as they felt they
were unable to hunt along with the rest of the group,
they'd ask to be helped to die.'

'What a gruesome thought!' shuddered Belinda.

'Selfless,' replied Mac. 'They put the good of the community first.'

Belinda paused. 'I only hope for their sakes it was quick.'

'There were two ways,' replied Mac. 'Either a leather
thong round the neck, a quick pull and——' he clicked
his tongue. 'Or a knife under the armpit.'

Belinda shuddered again.

'They're a tough people,' said Mac. 'They had to be,
to survive. That's why the government welfare is having
such a devastating effect on the old standards. If a man
knows that all he's got to do when winter comes is get
himself and his family into the nearest settlement in order
to qualify for a government hand-out, why should he risk
death to go hunting and trapping out in the snows?'

'You can understand it,' broke in Mrs Mac, 'but you
can see how demoralising it must seem, especially to the
older generation. Some people get quite heated about it.'
She shot a warning look at Mac. 'Politics always raises
the heat.'

Belinda smiled.

'It's difficult to think of political issues out here, but
when people's livelihoods and way of life are at stake I
suppose politics inevitably comes into it. But change is
bound to happen, isn't it? And surely it's better for the
natives to have whatever benefits of modern society they
can get?'

She imagined a brief echo of the dispute with Barron
earlier.

Mac was laughing and said teasingly, 'Some say the

benefits don't balance out the losses. That's an issue the politicians have to get their teeth into, not to mention the missionaries.' He chuckled to himself, and Belinda looked to Mrs Mac for explanation.

'There was an old couple down at Copper Bay when we first came out from England,' smiled Mrs Mac. 'Mac has never forgotten them. Whenever the chaplain made a visit, there they'd be, dutiful as ever, in church. But when it came round to being baptised they wouldn't go anywhere near him. One day he decided to have it out with them. "Why is it," he asked, "you come to all my services, you appear to enjoy them, yet you won't be converted?" The couple explained, "If we get baptised we'll have to do as you do." The chaplain was puzzled by this, so the woman said, "We all know how you frown on exchange mates. If we are baptised we'd no longer be able to exchange." Then she started to laugh. "It must be very boring when you can only have one man."'

Mrs Mac herself chuckled.

'I don't think things have changed much in that respect, have they, Mac?'

'You mean they still have open marriages?' asked Belinda curiously.

'According to what they print in the newspapers these days, the outside world's caught up with them,' chuckled Mac.

Belinda pondered on this. She wondered fleetingly what comment Derek would make. She looked slowly from one to the other. 'What if someone decided to go native——'

Mac gave a short laugh. 'For some that custom would be a mighty powerful incentive.' He laughed again.

'In the old days,' said Mrs Mac, giving her husband a rather reproving look, 'it was a practical sort of arrangement, because once couples were linked by an exchange they were duty bound to help each other out, to share whatever food they managed to trap. It was really a question of survival. Also it seemed to me that even the exchange couples were surprisingly faithful to each other. A link like that would last for maybe up to two years. There was nothing casual about it.'

'That's true,' said Mac, supporting what his wife had just said. 'There's a very practical attitude to life here. Life for anyone living in the old way is a precarious business. A hunter wouldn't last long without a woman. He needs somebody to stitch his clothes and boots and keep everything in good repair. Equipment in poor shape can mean the difference between life and death. That makes for a very special bond between man and woman. If you're out on the ice all day you really rely on somebody being back in camp to supervise the cooking, again, because proper nourishment can mean the difference between life and death.'

Belinda nodded. She could see the sense in that. But only if people were living in the old way. 'I can see that,' she said, 'but what about romance, what about——' she bit her lip, 'what about falling in love?'

Mrs Mac smiled. 'The young people seem to want that now, just like young folk anywhere else. Yes, things are changing in that respect, don't you agree, Mac?'

Mac grunted. 'I'll leave speculation of that sort to you women,' he said, knocking his pipe out on the fender and rooting about in his pockets for more tobacco. He leaned forward when he was settled with his pipe once more. 'It all comes down to context,' he said. 'What people do, how they behave, you've got to see it in the context of their environment. No looking down your nose because somebody's ways aren't yours. It's how well you survive in your environment that counts. That's all there is to it.' With this, he settled back again.

Belinda looked at him with slight misgivings. That was all very well, but when the needs of survival became less urgent, what then? Wasn't there then more freedom of choice? Couldn't a person choose how to conduct their life? What standards they would have? Her mind went fleetingly back to the incident in the wood yesterday, to the image of the young girl, scarcely more than a child, her arms full of furs, a cry of greeting on her lips. What sort of bond was it that had brought her and Barron together?

She got up irritably and wandered over to the radio receiver.

It looked as if she was momentarily back to playing the waiting game, and it was something she did not take kindly to by any means. After yesterday's argy-bargy with that man she was determined to go it alone, and already she had taken steps to enlist the help of Taqaq as a guide. She had also managed to persuade Mac to contact the air charter company. Not that that had taken much doing, with Mrs Mac smiling purposeful encouragement in the background. Mac had been promptly pushed in front of the transmitter and told to contact the station at Inuvik where Chuck and the private air charter company were based. He happened to be away on a job in the East, but would be returning in a day or two, and Mrs Mac had impressed on her husband the urgency of the message.

'Tell them. Go on, spell it out,' she had said. 'It's a matter of great urgency.'

Mac had complied without argument.

For another reason, namely the weather, it was a matter of urgency, and the recent report had done nothing to dissuade him of that fact. He had put his message in and now it was a question of waiting for a reply. When Chuck returned, he would fly Belinda out at once to a place on the Mackenzie River. There he would leave her and her guide, and with help from him she would travel by canoe to the place where the Nasaq had last been sighted. This was an old mining camp a couple of miles from the river, now practically defunct since the seam had proved less profitable than it had at first promised and the mining company had pulled out, leaving only one stubborn old prospector there. Trappers laying lines in the area would often drop in that way for a mug-up, and the chances were that old Sanderson would have heard something useful to pass on to Belinda.

'He's a prospector of the old school,' explained Mac. 'Adamantly refuses to have a transmitter installed, hates anything new-fangled. I don't know how he manages to eke out an existence.'

'He's a pigheaded old drunk, I'm afraid to say,' said Mrs Mac acerbically. 'I met him once down at Copper— lives like an animal, stuck in the past. He still dreams of the old days when a man could make a fortune overnight. But he's harmless enough, and his place is something of a meeting place at the head of the valley. Trappers always know they can get a drink there. If anybody knows anything, he should.'

'Take him a bottle of whisky and he'll tell you anything he can,' added Mac.

The idea was for Chuck to fly them north, leave them, then return in a couple of days after they'd had time to go on foot, have a word with Sanderson, sort something out if at all possible, then get back to the pick-up point on the river. Mac had been quite cheering. 'If they've gone to the ice fields that's the route they'll have taken, without a doubt, so at least you'll know one way or the other. If, as I'd guess, they're hunting caribou beyond the Mackenzie, then it'll be fairly easy to get word out through Sanderson.'

Belinda smiled wryly. 'So it'll be a question of wait and see again,' she said.

Mac had shrugged apologetically. 'If you're meant to meet them you will.' It was cold comfort, but it was all he could offer.

She fingered the knobs on the transmitter. Now she was counting the hours till she heard that Chuck was on his way. Restlessly she moved about the sitting-room. 'All right,' she said, 'I'll go and get some exercise and fresh air. Let me know straight away if any news comes through.' She pulled on her parka and in a few minutes was walking briskly in the frosty air towards the water's edge. One or two people were coming up the track and she exchanged a brief greeting with them. For once she wanted to rest from her struggles with the language and she walked briskly on. There was an air of unusual activity in the camp today, and she put it down to the preparations being made for the big freeze-up. No doubt everyone else was taking a leaf out of old Nuallataq's book too, and the knowledge made it even more important that she should get on to the next stage of her quest as soon as possible. Down by the stores there was a knot of people and she quickened her pace. May as well have a brief look at what's going on, she thought, then continue my exercise. Life is uneventful enough at the moment.

As she approached she saw that there was a team of dogs staked in an open space near the building and three or four men were standing around discussing something with a lot of hand gestures and much shrugging of the shoulders. It was obviously something pretty important. Belinda was wary of going too close. She had seen her first dog-team earlier in the week when one of the trappers from the north had come into camp, and she had been scared half out of her wits by the menacingly wild behaviour of the animals. Even as she watched, one of them started up a fight with the brute nearest to it and the owner of the team shouted angrily and gave the animal a cuff on the nose with his fist. The brute dropped its head and growled savagely, but it kept its teeth out of its companion for the time being. At that moment there was a commotion at the far end of the track which brought the group of men fanning out, faces turned expectantly towards the noise.

A fresh team came tearing boisterously round the corner of the store pulling a small wooden sled over the frozen ground. Belinda recognised the driver of the team at once and involuntarily stepped back a pace or two. But Barron was too intent on managing the dozen or so unruly dogs to let his glance wander elsewhere. With a few short, sharp commands he brought the fierce-looking mob to a halt, threw the hitching rope over a stake and swung easily off the sled. The men clustered round his tall figure, obviously eager to hear him give his verdict, and he replied fluently to their apparent questioning. One of the dogs was unhitched from its fellows and Barron took hold of it, digging his fingers into its thick hair as if examining it. It seemed to meet with his approval, because he said something to one of the men and a laugh and a burst of excited chatter broke out among them. Barron released the dog, but still holding its leash, took it to a corner of the building where there was a bundle lying on the ground. When he returned to the men he was slowly drawing through his hands a white fox fur—Belinda could see its shining luxury even at a distance. She gulped with amazement as Barron handed the fur to one of the men. In the city such a luxurious-looking object would fetch a high price. Now, as if a business deal had been successfully transacted, the two men briefly touched hands and Belinda watched fascinated as the Eskimo stuffed the fur into a bag on his back and made towards his team of dogs.

Something must have happened then, for, as the man walked close by the neighbouring team, one of the dogs suddenly leaped up at him, fastening its teeth savagely into the sleeve of the man's parka. It was the signal for all hell to break loose. Dogs from both teams erupted in a biting, yapping mêlée. The man fell to the ground and disappeared under the great furry bodies of the snarling half-breeds. In a flash, Barron had snatched up a stick and was wading in amongst the animals, lashing out at the ringleaders, striving desperately to bring the savage beasts under control. Two of the other men, after a moment's hesitation, managed to plunge in after Barron and drag the other man to safety.

Thanks to the thickness of his deerskin garments and

Barron's alacrity in getting the ringleaders under control, he seemed relatively unhurt, but Belinda found that she had rushed forward with a small cry of concern. She was now standing within a few feet of the place where Barron, having asserted his domination over the team, was calmly trying to untangle the lead reins. It was all over almost as soon as it had started, the dogs grizzling and growling among themselves, but otherwise calm. Belinda was trembling foolishly when the man turned to look at her. One of them came over to her at once, and she recognised him as a friend of Taqaq. He shrugged and gestured back to the dogs, making a sound in the back of his throat. His teeth flashed in a reassuring smile and he said something that Belinda could not understand.

Barron, easing his shoulders after his exertions, strode slowly over to them. 'He says there's nothing to be worried about. He thinks you look scared.'

'I'm not scared,' retorted Belinda at once. 'They are tied up, after all.' She tossed her head.

'That's all right, then,' replied Barron easily. His cold eyes swept her body once again, fastening on the parka she was wearing. Then abruptly he turned away. It was their first encounter in several days, and the first time he had spoken to her since she had said those insulting things in his house.

One of the men now said something to him and Barron went over to the dog which had caused all the trouble in the first place. Taking out a dangerous-looking long-bladed knife from his belt, he deftly cut the animal free from the rest of the team and dragged it with some difficulty to the man. To Belinda's horror the man produced a rifle from the equipment piled up outside the store, and before she knew what was happening he had knelt down beside the dog and shot it quickly and without another word in the head. Belinda's eyes dilated with shock and she stood for a long moment looking down at the now motionless mound of fur lying on the ground.

Barron had released it almost as the shot rang out and he was turning now back to his own recent acquisition, letting the dead animal's leash fall to the ground.

A sick feeling started in Belinda's stomach and rose to her throat. She could not take her eyes off the pathetic heap of fur. Then suddenly, as if galvanised into life, she sprang forward, her fists bunched, eyes blazing, cheeks crimson with rage. 'You've killed it!' she yelled at Barron. 'You knew he was going to shoot it. You've killed it—you savage!' She rushed up to Barron, prepared to do who knew what, but when he swung suddenly round to face her and she met the full impact of those ice blue eyes she faltered. More quietly she said, 'Why on earth did you do that?'

Barron rose to his full height. 'It was necessary,' he replied shortly. Then, as if she was of no more consequence than one of the animals he had subdued, he turned back to the men.

Belinda stood there trembling from head to foot. Her knees felt weak and her heart was beating madly in her breast as if it would never slow down. Her voice when it came was a croak of emotion. 'Necessary?' she asked. Barron didn't turn. She felt herself propelled forward by some force. 'Necessary?' she repeated, her voice regaining some of its former strength. 'What sort of twisted logic makes it necessary to shoot a dog on impulse?' She paused, willing him to turn, to explain himself.

He must have felt the force of her will, for, taking his time over it, he at length turned to face her. 'Dogs are like people,' he said, with a cruel smile. 'When they're young and new to the job they're apt to be nervous and excitable, ignorant too. They'll pull against the harness and bolt at the wrong times. They cause a man endless trouble. But once they realise who's boss they eventually settle down. Now and then you get an animal that won't do as it's told. It's either a loafer, or it's too unpredictable.' He shrugged. 'Such an animal is no use. It has to be shot.'

'But that's——' Belinda searched for a word which would sum up the full measure of her repugnance.

'If you give a dog a good hiding and it still doesn't behave——' he shrugged, 'that's the way it has to be,' he finished emphatically, and again made as if to go.

Belinda moved forward. She didn't know what she wanted to say. There was no point in arguing with such a man. Yet she felt a desperate need to continue the dialogue. 'Have you killed many dogs?'

Even as the words were uttered, she heard the cold contempt in her voice, and hesitated again.

But Barron at once swung into the attack. 'Oh, hundreds,' he said sarcastically. 'I'm known as the local butcher. And not just dogs,' he added dangerously. 'You must have heard of my reputation by now. After all, what is the law out here? A man can behave as he wishes. Anything goes in the name of survival.' His lips drew back in a brief, hard smile. 'You must feel very much out of place in a country of such barbarians,' he went on contemptuously. 'Next time you must be more careful where you choose to take your annual holiday. A package deal to Disneyland would be something more in your line.'

'I——' the words of protest remained unspoken. With a sudden cry of anger, Belinda had shot out her hand before she could stop it, and hit him square and hard in the face. For a moment nothing happened. The thought flashed into her mind that she had merely dreamed it. But the tell-tale colour darkening Barron's tanned cheek, the imprint of her fingers across the side of his face, belied this fancy, and she let her breath come out in a long sigh of resignation. Now she had really done it! She realised that a man like this would have no qualms about hitting a woman. She waited, beyond fear, for some retaliation. Surely the other men would step in. They would protect her from the full brunt of his wrath. She waited. Barron was still standing erect in front of her. His eyes seemed to become hooded, his hands hung limply at his side. Slowly, as if in a dream, she noted the bunched muscles of his shoulders, the broad well-developed chest, the athletically slim waist and narrow hips, the firm masculine stance, the overall huskiness of the man.

'Oh, I'm sorry——' she breathed when at last she could speak. 'I didn't mean——' Her words tailed off. It was no good adding lies to injury. She didn't feel sorry at all. She thought he deserved it. And anyway, apologies would leave a desperado like him unmoved.

She became aware of the sounds around them—the still grizzling animals, the suddenly hushed conversation of the men as they too waited expectantly for Barron to react. She was dimly aware of one or two smiles and she groaned inwardly at the thought that this latest confrontation, built on a series of earlier incidents, was more than just an isolated event, that could be glossed over. But she stood her ground.

Barron slowly moved towards her, but her eyes rounded as, instead of raising his hand to strike her, he grasped her firmly by the shoulders and began to propel her towards the store. She tried to pull away, but like the reluctant animal he had picked out from the team, she was forced to submit to his superior strength. Without a word he half dragged, half carried her around the corner of the building out of sight of the men. Only when they were alone did he speak.

'I would like to have done this in full view of them all, but I do have some respect for convention, despite what you think.' And with that, she felt his breath on her forehead, then his lips were coming down hard on her own. With a shudder she felt the hard-packed muscles of his body crushing her against the wall of the store and with sharp little animal moans she tried frantically to break herself free. It was hopeless. Her strength was no match for his. She found she was fighting for breath, moving her head desperately from side to side, but his lips little by

little increased their pressure, forcing her mouth open.
Tears of humiliation began to appear in the corners of
her eyes so that in a sudden access of despair she brought
her teeth hard together on to his lower lip. It was a mis-
take. Now they were alone there was no constraint on
him, and he did not hesitate to retaliate, forcing her head
back against the wooden wall of the store as his powerful
jaw worked bruisingly over her face, hungrily searching
for some sign of response. Against her will, Belinda felt
her body tremble in answer to his urgent demand. She
felt her limbs turn to putty in his hands and despite herself
she heard herself moaning in ecstasy against him.

After what seemed like eternity, Barron gently released
her, and for a moment or two they leaned breathlessly
against each other like survivors of a tornado. Slowly the
reality of what had happened came sweeping in on
Belinda and with a little movement she pushed him away.
For a moment she was conscious of his steady gaze, the
strange glitter in the depths of his blue eyes.

'Now you've got what you asked for,' his eyes mocked
her. 'You didn't even have to come to my hut this time.'
She felt his fingers digging into her arms and angrily tried
to struggle free. 'The primitive may have a limited appeal
for some. I think you're an exception to that rule.' His
lips twisted into a smile.

'How dare you!' Her voice shook with hopelessly mixed
emotion. She still burned from the touch of his body, but
the cold mockery in his eyes stung her pride and she was
swept along in a torrent of rage. 'I hate you!' she spat.
'You're the most hateful, arrogant man I've ever met!'
His answer was to bring his lips crushingly down again on
her own. 'Oh, Barron,' she moaned when she managed to
free her mouth for a moment. 'Don't, don't! I don't
want——' Her words were stopped again by his hungry
lips and she gave herself to the ecstasy of the moment.

Suddenly she felt his body withdraw and his grip
slackened so suddenly that she fell back abruptly against

the side of the store. For a moment she was dazed and looked round in bewilderment. Barron had stepped back and there was a hard, cold gleam in his eyes. His face seemed to twist into a sneer as he gave a short, unamused laugh. 'You're so different, aren't you?' he sneered sarcastically. 'You wouldn't barter your body for anything. No!' he laughed derisively. 'You'd give it away as casually as——'

'Don't!' Her cry was high and anguished. 'I hate you! You don't know me! You're the last person I'd ever give anything to. You?' Her voice was harsh, but she was in a turmoil of pain and humiliation and longing. Not quite knowing what she was doing, she began to beat on his chest with her fists and he was so surprised it was a minute before he managed to control her flailing arms. For a moment he crushed her body up against his own again before pushing her angrily away. Tears of anger and frustration sprang into her eyes, and she stood panting before him. 'You're the most hateful man I've ever met!' she cried again.

Barron's lips curled. 'You asked for it,' he jibed. 'You've taken on more than you can cope with mixing with me. I'm not some effete boy you can play games with.'

With a little cry Belinda began to make her way, stumbling a little, with averted glance, back round the side of the building. How could she have responded so readily to the brute's hateful advances? She ran her fingers shakily through her dishevelled hair. What on earth had come over her, to behave in this idiotic manner? Now he would despise her even more. And with just cause, she thought grimly, allowing him to do that, roughly and without feeling, like an animal. Burning waves of self-disgust brought bright colour to her cheeks.

She walked reluctantly to where the men were still chatting, her eyes downcast. Fortunately they were occupied with their dogs and she noted dully that the shot animal was still lying where it had fallen. With a

shudder of confused emotion she began to make her way
back up the path to the house. So much for the energetic
walk she had planned in order to take her mind off things!
Now her thoughts were once again thrown into a turmoil
by this man. Without looking back she made her way up
to the house.

It was three days later that word at last came through
from the charter company. Chuck was already on his way.
All being well, he should touch down later that morning.
Belinda eyed the landing strip with trepidation from her
vantage point at the kitchen window. There was certainly
no problem with mud now. After the heavy rainfall soon
after her arrival, the weather had been bitterly cold with
a continuous heavy frost. Already the ground was
hardened like rock and gave a foretaste of the winter to
come. The packed earth of the landing strip was like con-
crete now. The previous three days had been spent in
constant nervous activity, checking and double-checking
the equipment they were to take out to Sanderson's claim.
Belinda had decided to take her recording equipment just
in case they should strike lucky at once, and there was
also a supply of provisions should they have to fall back
on their own resources. Standard emergency rations, Mac
told her. It was with much anxiety that she now contemplated the journey—not only because Sanderson's place
wasn't even a dot on the map, but because the latest incident with Barron had thoroughly unnerved her.
Suddenly the vulnerability of her position in this lawless
country had begun to dawn on her. Difficult though it
was to fathom Barron's motives in so humiliating her, it
was not pleasant to contemplate what might have
happened in different circumstances when his passions
might not have been so easily restrained by the presence
of other men.

She was reassured of Taqaq's reliability, both by the
confidence Mac showed in him and by the fact that he

had shown her nothing but courtesy in all their meetings. She had remained close to the main building, busy anyhow with her preparations, but also anxious to avoid any further contact with Barron.

The track from the lake passed right in front of the house and led up to the far end of the settlement where it wound past a row of prefabricated dwellings and gradually petered out in a network of little paths among the tents and temporary shelters of those who were simply in camp to pick up supplies and renew old contacts. Once or twice Belinda had seen Barron going along this path, but she had been careful each time to keep well out of sight. Nor had she been able to discern the nature of his errand. She assumed it was something to do with the girl Ikluk, and knowing what she now did of some of the native customs she was surprised that they did not live together. She assumed that this was because the girl was already married, although she had never seen her with any other man. Fortunately Barron never seemed to visit the house, and except for the time when he had come into the stores to buy new traplines, he seemed to keep his relationship with the Macdonalds to a minimum.

Now she scanned the unchanging grey of the low-lying cloud with anxious eyes, searching for the speck in the sky which would be the means of her temporary deliverance from this place. Even a few days' respite would be welcome, she told herself. The knowledge that that hateful man was so close by was abhorrent to her. She felt oppressed by the very thought of his presence, of what he must be thinking about her, if indeed he bothered to give her a second's thought now that she had made it clear that she was unwilling to give in to him. She sighed, impatient with herself, and idly drew a figure on the misted kitchen window. She rubbed it out angrily. This waiting was really getting on her nerves. Derek had not warned her of any of this.

For the rest of the morning she forced herself to keep

busy by yet again rechecking the things she had decided
to take with her out to Sanderson's. There was little
enough, but at least it was some form of occupation.
Under Mac's guidance she had been down to the store
and earmarked a dozen or so gas drums, two small stoves,
a couple of grub boxes and some dehydrated provisions.
Mac had suggested she also take a supply of dried caribou
meat, and, unlocking his liquor store that morning, he
had insisted on pressing a bottle of whisky into her hands
as a bargaining counter for old Sanderson. As well as this,
she had sleeping bags, one each for herself and Taqaq,
and a small storm tent. 'Not that you'll be needing that,'
said Mac reassuringly, 'it's only a morning's walk from
the creek, but it'd be foolhardy not to be properly
equipped for any emergency at this time of year.' Once
again he had reassured her of Taqaq's skill at manipulat-
ing the kayak through the tricky waters of the Mackenzie
tributary, and she had thrust all doubt on that score to
one side when she had watched him manoeuvring about
the choppy waters of the inlet as to the manner born.
Mac had reassured her that there were no real rapids on
that particular stretch of river and that it was merely the
uneven nature of the land around Sanderson's claim that
made it impractical to attempt a landing in such a place.
'Hardly worth risking lives when a short river journey
and half a morning's trek inland will do the job almost as
quickly,' he said. Belinda made a real effort to put her
worries aside.

For the umpteenth time that morning she was checking
the store of dried food, the tea, the cocoa, the dried milk
and so on and, deeply engrossed as she was, it was only
when Mrs Mac came bustling into the porch where the
gear was temporarily stored, with her face wreathed in
smiles, that Belinda noticed the unaccustomed sound of a
single-engined plane approaching. With a gasp of delight
she sprang to her feet and followed Mrs Mac outside.

Sure enough, bursting through the low ceiling of cloud

was a small aircraft. It was Chuck's familiar Anson rapidly making a checking circuit before coming into land.

He seemed to see the women at once, for his port wing dipped, then he was pulling the plane up and heading back at speed towards the landing strip. It was all Belinda could do not to throw herself into his arms as, after the engine had finally died, the familiar figure swung down from the cockpit and came loping over the hard-packed earth towards her. His boyish face gave away more than he realised as he came towards her and when he was within speaking distance he called out some pleasantry, cuffing her playfully on the shoulder when he got into the lee of the house.

'You don't look any different,' he told her, swinging his grip down beside him.

'Should I?' she replied with a laugh.

'It just seems a mighty long time, that's all,' he answered, shrugging his shoulders awkwardly.

He turned away quickly and made some show of going inside, shouting noisy hellos to everyone. A group of Eskimos had already come over to the main house to see him and he exchanged boisterous greeting with them, obviously pleased to meet old acquaintances, but also glad to be able to conceal his feelings on meeting up with Belinda again.

Belinda herself was eager to get away, and within an hour or so the plane had been loaded up, the kayak carried aboard, and the Macs were standing beaming on the front, having a few last-minute words with Chuck.

Taqaq was already on board, eager for a break in routine, and looking forward to seeing some relatives of his who hunted around Sanderson's claim, so he told Belinda. Chuck was just about to walk away from the Macs when Belinda happened to glance down the path to the beach, and gave an involuntary shudder. Barron, fur hood pulled up against the biting wind, was walking purposefully towards the little knot of people around the plane. Fear seemed to grip Belinda's heart irrationally when she caught sight of him, and calling out to Chuck, she began to make her way hurriedly across the landing strip. The last thing she wanted was to come face to face with Barron.

However, before she could get even half-way to the aircraft, she heard a voice call 'Belinda!'

She froze on the spot. It was the first time he had used her name. She was even surprised that he knew it. Now she steeled herself for some fresh encounter, and with an impatient toss of her head she turned to meet him.

'Yes?' she enquired peremptorily.

His eyes pierced her own and she felt a flush of colour sweep her body. The lips which had searched hers so hungrily were compressed in a tight disapproving line. 'This is crazy,' he snapped. 'I've just heard where you're going. Macdonald must be mad to let you go up there at this time of year!'

Belinda turned scornfully on her heel. 'You'll do anything to stop me meeting them, won't you? But you won't succeed. When I make up my mind to do a thing, I jolly well do it!' She looked back at him with tight lips. 'I asked you for help and you refused. That's the end as far as I'm concerned. There are plenty of people who will help and,' she added for good measure, 'without being asked either.'

She turned abruptly on her heel, glad to see that Chuck had at last said his goodbyes and was setting out across the strip. Belinda had made a couple of steps towards the Anson when she felt a hand come out and spin her round.

'I tell you it's madness,' said Barron tightly.

Belinda closed her eyes in studied impatience. 'I can't say I'm terribly interested in your opinion,' she replied. 'We've listened to the weather reports. There's nothing to stop us. It's an ideal time to go. Now will you please take your hands off me.' She paused.

Barron went on gripping her by the arm so that her

eyes blazed angrily. 'You're hurting me,' she said coldly. She was relieved to feel his grip go slack. 'I wonder what's so special about these people, your so-called friends, that you have to make such a fuss about them,' she said.

'It's nothing like that,' broke in Barron impatiently. 'Go and see them. If you can find them,' he added ominously. 'They've heard all about you.'

Belinda paused. 'No doubt you've warned them off,' she threw back, tartly. 'I wouldn't put anything past you!'

Just then Chuck approached. He threw a tight-lipped glance at Barron before deliberately taking Belinda by the elbow and ushering her to the ladder leading up into the cockpit. Barron made a move forward, then checked himself. He looked quickly back at the people standing by the building ready to wave their goodbyes, then he moved quickly in front of Chuck, barring the way with his body. He leaned nonchalantly on the ladder and gazed steadily into the pilot's face.

'Have you thought this out, Robinson?' he asked.

Chuck's reddish hair didn't bely the quickness of his temper. 'I fly where I'm chartered to fly. Now get out of my way,' he snapped fiercely, making as if to push Barron aside. The taller of the two men laughed softly. 'Don't try it kid.' As if to emphasise his contempt for the younger man, he put both his hands deep in the pockets of his parka and lolled back against the ladder as if he had all the time in the world. Chuck glowered but checked.

'What's the game? Come on, out with it!' he snarled. Belinda blurted that he was trying to prevent her from meeting the Nasaq.

'Is that true?' demanded Chuck. Barron took his time in answering. He looked up at the sky, westwards, then meaningfully back at Chuck. The boy coloured angrily. 'We've got plenty of time. These people at the weather station know a damned sight more than——' he stopped, conscious of Taqaq who had come to the door of the cockpit to see what the excitement was about. He tried a more reasonable approach. 'Look,' he said, vainly trying to take Barron by the arm and lead him off to one side. 'It's a couple of hundred miles up north. They'll be gone a few days. I don't know why there's all this fuss.'

He fell back as Barron jerked his arm violently away and angrily made as if to follow up with a punch. Belinda allowed a cry to escape her, but abruptly Barron stepped back from the ladder and started to make off across the strip in the direction of the settlement without another word. Chuck watched him go, wearing a puzzled expression which didn't change when he shot a glance at Belinda's flushed face. With a hundred questions burning behind his eyes he began to climb the ladder. At the top he turned to look down at her. 'Well?' he demanded. 'Coming with us?' Pulling herself together, Belinda climbed up and found her seat beside him.

He didn't gun the engines at once but sat for a moment, his eyes fixed moodily on some view out of the cockpit window. Then quietly, his boyish face striving to conceal the emotions that struggled there, he turned to Belinda.

'What was all that about?' he asked.

Belinda glanced briefly across the strip. Barron hadn't waited like the others. His tall figure was already striding athletically towards the prefabs. Going to see his young girl-friend, she surmised. She lowered her eyes and gave a little sigh, and her voice was apologetic when she spoke. 'It seems I've got on his wrong side. I told you, he doesn't want me to meet the Nasaq. It seems as if he'll stop at nothing to prevent it.' This seemed to suffice, for Chuck started the engine up and Belinda was thankful to find that, as at the beginning, conversation was impossible above the din.

CHAPTER SIX

By the time the plane was coming in to land on the spit at the edge of the Mackenzie tributary, Chuck's earlier subdued manner had given way to his usual boisterous good humour. He and Belinda had managed to exchange one or two words at the tops of their voices about the terrain over which they were flying, and Belinda was relieved to see that he held no jealous grudge against her. Now the plane was bucking across the landing strip and she was putting all her energy into simply holding on to her seat, despite the restraining safety harness which Chuck had insisted she fasten up before he put the plane into its approach run. When they at last got down out of the plane they walked about for a moment, stretching their legs, taking in great gulps of Arctic air, and becoming a little lightheaded with the invigorating clarity of so much oxygen. Taqaq was plainly excited to be so near to meeting his family once again and began to unload the gear from the aircraft straightaway. Together he and Chuck lifted the kayak down to the water's edge and while Chuck lashed the painter firmly to a stake on the makeshift wooden jetty, Taqaq went back to the plane and began to set about transferring the equipment from it into the kayak.

'I'll take the recording gear,' said Belinda hurriedly, clucking nervously around it as Taqaq swung the box with her cassettes, batteries, notebooks and precious recorder down on to the rocky ground. She lifted the modern lightweight equipment easily under one arm and returned to the landing place.

Chuck looked up with an easy grin. 'We always seem

to be in transit,' he said. 'When are we going to have time for a good long chat?'

Belinda smiled coquettishly. 'If you will spend all your time flying around the Arctic,' she said, 'what can I do about it? I've been kicking my heels in Two Rivers for the last three weeks. You should have taken your chance then.'

'I've got some holiday leave coming up soon,' he told her, suddenly serious. 'Might you be thinking of taking a few days' rest soon yourself? You'll surely finish this job within the week?'

Belinda paused. 'I've been so taken up with the search for these people, I hadn't really thought how long it would take to get the recordings I need,' she told him. 'If they co-operate I want to spend as long as I can—maybe several weeks, living with them, travelling with them if they'll allow it, getting as much information as I can on to those cassettes.' She indicated the box containing the recording equipment. 'I can't think of days off till I've carried out my assignment.'

Seeing the brief look of disappointment in his face, she took him impulsively by the arm. 'I hope we can meet some time without the noise of that damned Anson drowning out our voices. It's giving me a sore throat.'

Chuck gave her a sudden hug. 'Look,' he said, 'take care, won't you? Don't do anything silly.' He released her slowly as Taqaq approached.

'Are you going back right now?' asked Belinda, her mouth turning down at the corners at the thought of his imminent departure.

' 'fraid so. I'll have to leave while the light still holds,' he replied. 'I'd stay if I could.' For a moment his eyes began to calculate, then he shrugged. 'No chance, though. They'll be sending out search parties if I don't turn up on schedule. Wait till I have my own charter company. While I'm under contract like this I'm nothing but a wage slave.'

Belinda laughed. The idea of Chuck being any kind of slave was novel, and she said so.

He turned his back so that Taqaq couldn't see him. Then he bent towards her, a lock of curly reddish hair falling over his forehead. 'I'm a slave all right,' he told her. 'Just whistle and see who'll come running!'

Belinda lowered her eyes. He was a dear, sweet boy. She felt flattered that he should feel this way about her after so short an acquaintance. Any girl would be pleased by his attentions. For a moment she didn't say anything, and when she did she tried to speak lightly.

'Just tell me again,' she said. 'We've got three full days to search these people out. And on the fourth day,' she paused, 'that's when you'll touch down here to pick us up?'

'Yes,' he answered. 'Try and make it by mid-morning. You'll be travelling down river, so it'll be a pretty swift return journey. I'll land here on the spit and hang about until you show. We'll decide what to do next depending on what happens up at old Sanderson's place. If you draw a blank, it'll be back to the settlement——'

'Don't say that!' broke in Belinda impatiently. 'I won't draw a blank. I can't!'

'Well,' replied Chuck calmly, 'I'm simply crossing off the least likely possibility first.'

Belinda glanced quickly at him. She was trying to judge whether he was simply saying that to keep her happy, but he was already going on. 'Or, if you hear that they're hereabouts in the vicinity, out towards the west, say, I can take you there. I'm keeping two days after our rendezvous free and open for you to dispose of as you wish.' He grinned at her. 'I don't have to tell you I'm hoping you'll put them to mutually pleasurable use.'

'Yes, Chuck,' grinned Belinda, 'but let's keep things on a businesslike footing for a moment, shall we? What happens if I get to know something about them but can't get out to them by air? I've had a look at the map and it

seems that a lot of the land over to the north and east, in
fact on their possible route to the snowfields, is rocky and
pretty unsuitable for landing a light aircraft on. So what
then?'

Chuck looked troubled. 'We'll cross that bridge if and
when we get to it. Mac impressed on me the importance
of keeping our rendezvous in three days' time. If the
Nasaq are holed up somewhere, somewhere where it's
impossible for me to land, it might be on the cards to get
up there by kayak, or to entice them down to Sanderson's.
The last one is your best bet,' he added. 'They're used to
travelling over this sort of terrain and they're equipped
for it.'

'But how would I manage to get word to them that I'd
like them to come down here?'

'Send Taqaq if there's no one else passing through,'
replied Chuck at once, 'he'll be able to travel quickly if
he's by himself, and he's a good, reliable guide.'

'Then I'll have to stay at Sanderson's alone.' Belinda
wrinkled her brow.

'Maybe not quite alone,' replied Chuck. 'Let it ride.
See what you find out. You're not pushed for time. As
long as you're out of this place before the snows come,
you can take it easy. If you can locate them and maybe
even get word out that you want to see them and can
travel, these few days won't be wasted. They can come
down from wherever they are at present by sled when the
freeze comes. They can cover thirty-odd miles a day, even
eighty or so when the going's good. If that doesn't work
you can always arrange another expedition when you
know where you're supposed to be headed.'

'That's true,' said Belinda with a thoughtful smile. 'I
suppose I'm still in too much of a hurry—desperate to
meet non-existent deadlines! It's a bad habit. It's just that
I want to meet them now, this moment, not in several
weeks' time! I want to get the job started. I feel as if I've
been marking time since I arrived out here. When I

accepted the assignment I had no idea it was going to take so long simply to establish contact. I thought it was going to be like getting on a train and making sure I got off at the right stop. When Derek said they were nomadic I didn't really give a thought to what that actually meant.' She smiled ruefully. 'Things are so strange here, so different from the way they are in England. All this space,' she waved her hand around to include the many miles of uninhabited rock-strewn tundra which seemed to enclose them in a strange intimacy. 'A person could easily get lost in it, could travel for weeks without ever seeing a living soul. It's difficult to adjust to it. And it's weird too, this having no need to look at a clock from sun-up to nightfall, to let life simply take its own time.'

'You've got one deadline to meet,' said Chuck, taking her hand and raising the finger tips to his lips. 'It's important. The freeze-up doesn't hold off for anybody. You'll have half the rescue services out if you're not here to time.' He brushed her fingers lightly with his lips and added, 'As well as one very worried air charter pilot!'

For a moment Belinda thought he was going to kiss her, but with a sudden deepening of colour, he turned briskly away. 'I'd best be getting back before dark,' he said huskily. 'Let's check the equipment on board.'

Taqaq had made a good job of loading the kayak in what seemed to his expert eye the safest and most efficient manner. All that was left to do now was for Belinda to climb aboard and settle herself on the thwart amidships. Chuck hung about on the landing stage until they were ready to go, then he untied the painter and Taqaq was suddenly swinging the bows of the canoe into the turbulent waters of the mainstream. The last view Belinda had of Chuck, he was raising one hand in farewell. Then they were quickly caught up in the rushing waters and all her attention became focussed on the bucking and plunging of the boat.

It was true what Mac had said about Taqaq's skill and

also, Belinda thankfully noted, about the absence of rapids on this stretch of the river. After the initial shock of being waterborne in the flimsy native craft, she began to enjoy the adventure of it all. The water wasn't swift enough to cause any real problems and Taqaq paddled easily and rhythmically, guiding the laden vessel expertly between the rocky banks.

Belinda lost track of time in the dreamy half-light of the overcast sky, but it must have been after about an hour or so when they finally came to a widening in the river and Taqaq steered the kayak into the shallows where a shelving cobbled beach gave access on to the bank. Without too much difficulty he managed to pull the kayak on to the edge to allow Belinda to climb out without getting too wet. Taqaq himself waded up to his thighs, long sealskin boots protecting him from the wet. He managed to swing the stern of the kayak into safe mooring and together they lifted the boat up on to dry land. It was now that Belinda saw the reason for keeping their equipment to the minimum. Within a few minutes they had unloaded it all, strapped it on to their backs and, with Taqaq leading the way, set off along a faintly outlined track into the hinterland.

Belinda noticed that Taqaq carried a large knife tucked into his belt and within easy reach of his hand, and when she asked him if he carried it for any special reason, he smiled with a flash of gleaming teeth and explained that sometimes there would be bear and it was always wise to go armed in such regions. Belinda questioned the possibility of attack, her palms, she noticed irritably, becoming suddenly clammy inside their fur mittens. Taqaq shrugged and said that perhaps it wasn't likely, and anyway bear would have to be disturbed before attacking and they were both to move carefully. He flashed another grin at her. 'This knife wouldn't be much protection anyway,' he told her. Belinda shuddered, not sure if he was teasing her or not, but when she tried to say this to Taqaq he just smiled

and walked steadily onwards. Belinda wondered if his
English was as good as Mac had claimed, but it was difficult to carry on a conversation when they were walking
in single file through such an oppressive silence.

It was fortunately only a short walk. In a little time
they were heading towards a log cabin set at the foot of a
limestone crag sheltered on two sides by pine trees which
marked the beginnings of a deep valley. A water barrel
stood outside, and there was a washing line attached between two trees and other signs of what passed for dom-
esticity in this wild region.

Belinda hurried forward with a cry of relief. She had
not wanted to admit to herself the feeling of desolation
she had momentarily felt as she had been borne away
from the figure framed against the Anson, that little
symbol of safety and protection amidst the overpowering
threat of nature in the raw, and now she eagerly approached the big wooden door of the cabin with a cry of
greeting springing to her lips. To her mystification there
was no answering response. Together she and Taqaq
banged on the heavy door, then the Eskimo raised his
voice in a shout. But there was still no reply. With an
impatient push he gave the door his weight and it swung
open to reveal the main room of the cabin.

'Sanderson!' called Taqaq loudly. 'Visitors! Come on,
man! Where are you hiding?' He stepped inside, closely
followed by Belinda. She swung the heavy pack down off
her shoulders and peered round. It was a rough abode,
there was no doubt about that, with no trace of a woman's
hand to give it that homely touch. There was nothing but
an earth floor and uncut timbers to keep out the wind. A
large blackened stove dominated one wall, a dresser dis-
playing a few unmatched plates, a rough-hewn table and
chair comprised Sanderson's home. And then the sickly
sweet smell of alcohol and tobacco assailed them with a
pungency that was overwhelming after the clarity of the
air outside. Belinda felt a sudden tightening in her stom-

ach muscles, which made her remember that she hadn't
eaten since that morning. Mrs Mac had given her the full
works, even so it was a long time since and the combina-
tion of hunger and sudden fug made her want to retch.
She must have swayed, for Taqaq put out a steadying
hand. Together they strained their eyes, trying to make
out the shapes in the shadowy room. One thing was sure
in the rapidly failing light—there was a stack of empty
whisky bottles laid up against the wall right by where
they stood that would have done justice to any Saturday
night party. Taqaq gave them an uninterested glance and
went on farther into the room.

'Hah! Sanderson!' he yelled suddenly, moving lightly
over to an untidy-looking couch pulled up in front of the
big black stove. It was facing away from the door, but
Taqaq, observant, had spied one boot-clad foot sticking
out over the arm. He went up to the couch and peered
cautiously over. Belinda saw him wrinkle his nose with
distaste, then it seemed as if the couch had come abruptly
alive, for something fur-clad and of enormous shape
seemed to rear up with a deep roar, and without thinking
Belinda had turned and started to head fast for the door.
Only when she heard a man's mumbling laugh and
Taqaq's cries of greeting did she pause to look back. Then
she saw the Eskimo back-slapping the shapeless figure
which had risen up at him from the couch. He was being
practically crushed in a huge bear-hug in return, but
somehow the dark-haired Taqaq managed to extricate
himself from Sanderson's hold on him, and by the time
the two men had finished she had already edged closer and
was standing open-mouthed as they turned to look at her.

'Well, well, well, what have we here, you old dark
horse, Taqaq! Hey?' The dishevelled old man with a bush
of tobacco-stained, once white beard nudged the young
Eskimo in the ribs, and Taqaq raised his arms helplessly
at Belinda.

'I'm a researcher from the university of——' began

Belinda, but the bear of a man cut in with a rumbling belly-laugh.

'Don't tell me——' he wheezed alcoholically, 'I've heard all about you.' He slowly began to subside on to the couch again. 'Have a drink,' he waved his arms expansively towards the half empty bottle on the floor beside him. 'I won't get up—bad leg.' He turned to Taqaq. 'Come on, man, get the little lady a drink.'

Grumbling and wheezing, he lay back among the grubby furs covering the couch.

Belinda looked at Taqaq. 'Shall we ask him now?'

Taqaq grimaced. Sanderson's eyes were already closed and he appeared oblivious to the presence of guests. 'Hey, Sanderson,' said Taqaq. 'Aren't you going to talk to us? We've come a long way to have a mug-up with you.'

Sanderson's eyes snapped open and he eyed the Eskimo shrewdly. 'I know why you're here,' he shot a glance in Belinda's direction. 'If you've anything of the man about you, Taqaq, you'll forget the Nasaq and enjoy yourself.'

Belinda blushed furiously, and even Taqaq looked uncomfortable. She smiled reassuringly at him. She knew why he was so eager to come out to the Hell's Gate region. He had already told her about the young Eskimo girl who was travelling in that region with her people. 'So you've heard about the Nasaq recently,' she put in smoothly. 'We heard they were maybe hunting around here——'

'Then you heard wrong,' said Sanderson, again shooting her a piercing glance from beneath furrowed brows. 'Pass the bottle, Taqaq, and stop shuffling about like that.' He reached out and took the bottle from Taqaq's hand and swigged it back. He wiped the neck politely and handed it to Belinda.

'I'll get you a—maybe not a glass,' grinned Taqaq, 'but something to drink it from.'

'I'm not sure I can cope with whisky on an empty stomach,' demurred Belinda.

Taqaq came close to her and said, out of the corner of his mouth, 'He's going to be difficult. Keep in his good books. O.K.?' He poured a small tot of the whisky into two none too clean mugs he found on the dresser and drawing up a chair for Belinda, made a space for himself on the couch.

'Well, man,' he started, 'how've you been keeping since I was last out this way?'

Sanderson retrieved the whisky bottle before answering. 'Had a visitor,' he said.

Taqaq looked at the whisky bottle with a nod. 'Looks like it,' he said. 'Anybody we know?'

'Somebody who knows your little friend,' wheezed Sanderson. He chuckled comfortably to himself. All at once he seemed to collapse in a wheezing heap among the furs. He seemed to fall asleep almost at once, snoring fiercely and unmusically, the bottle gripped tightly across his chest.

'Oh hell,' said Taqaq, 'we'll have to wait. No point in rousing a sleeping bear. Big trouble then, no?'

Belinda sighed. She saw the wisdom of Taqaq's remark, but was finding it difficult to conceal her impatience. Looking closer, and gingerly still holding the enamel mug into which Taqaq had apologetically poured a token drop of the whisky, she saw that old Sanderson was in fact quite a small man, barrel-shaped but short, with a wizened craggy face, darkened by wind and weather, as well as infrequent washing. He was almost completely bald with nothing but a fringing of yellowish hair at the back of his head. Tobacco stains yellowed the front of a dirty-looking shirt which seemed to be held together by a couple of safety pins, and an old dress waistcoat that had obviously seen better days completed the top half of his garb. His legs were encased in a pair of enormous trousers fastened at the waist with string, a pair of braces hanging down the front, fulfilling no particular function. Only the boots seemed cared for, although even they were old and had obviously seen better days.

Belinda took all this in with sinking heart. She hadn't
been unduly put off by Mrs Mac's description, because
she imagined that at least the man would be able to talk
to them, give them some sort of answer to their questions.
But this! He was obviously going to be no use whatsoever.
Her face must have shown her dismay, for Taqaq patted
her shoulder in a brotherly fashion.

'Chin up,' he said. 'Somebody got here before us with
the whisky. Wait till it wears off.'

'That might be ages,' replied Belinda.

Taqaq shrugged. 'I'll fix us something to eat. I know
this place. Many a time I have Sanderson's hospitality.'
He looked questioningly at Belinda. 'Is that the right
word—hospitality?'

Belinda couldn't help grinning. 'Yes, that's right. Arctic
hospitality is a variable experience.'

Having plunged straight into sleep Sanderson snored
throughout their meal. Belinda's mind was turning over
what Sanderson had said, but as he showed no sign of
coming to, she had no way of knowing that what she
suspected was true or merely the fancy of her imagination.
Eventually she looked up at Taqaq. 'It's obvious that he's
going to be no use to us,' she said, 'so what now?'

Taqaq poured another tot of whisky each. It was their
third or fourth now. At first it had hit her hard in the
stomach, but now it was beginning to fill her with a rosy
warmth. 'Maybe you'll have to call it a day.' Taqaq sat
back in his chair and regarded her thoughtfully.

'I can't give up. Not now.'

'Maybe you should wait here for a day or so, then make
your way back to the river. Somebody may come in in
that time.'

'I'm going to have to get a letter off to Derek as soon as
I get back to base.' She was thinking aloud now. 'No one
can say I haven't tried. As for hospitality, look at him!'

Taqaq wrinkled his face distastefully. With a rush,

Belinda asked the questions which had been burning inside her head throughout the meal. 'Who got here before us? Who told him about me? How did he know I wanted to meet the Nasaq?'

Taqaq's eyes were unfathomable as he gazed into the fire. 'There are many possibilities. At this time many people come out from the trading post, and they all know to spread the word. Mac told them.'

Belinda nodded. Perhaps she was letting her feelings cloud her judgment. She had had another and more unpleasant idea. But what Taqaq had said was probably true —anyone could have mentioned her quest to Sanderson. It was just that something in the way he had said it made it sound as if he had been warned not to give anything away. She put this thought tentatively to Taqaq.

'But why should anyone do that?' he laughed. 'It would be hard enough to meet them without putting traps in the way.' He poured another tot of whisky.

With a deep sigh Belinda let the anxiety drain out of her body. She had done what she could; now she would just have to wait. It was as if she was now entirely in the hands of fortune. For the present at least there was nothing more to be done.

A couple of hours later, serenaded by the still snoring prospector, Taqaq and Belinda were sitting at the kitchen table, playing gin rummy, the remains of an adequate meal of stew and dumplings still in front of them. Belinda was thinking that really it was quite pleasant to have given up looking for the Nasaq, even if only temporarily. The wind that had been steadily getting up through the day was now blowing with a frightening force around the cabin, but this just seemed to add to the cosiness inside. Apologetically Taqaq reached out for the unopened bottle.

'Are you going to get drunk, Taqaq?' Belinda asked disapprovingly.

'Not unless you are,' he quipped.

'I shall endeavour not to,' she answered primly.

Taqaq's teeth shone brightly in a quick smile. His dark hair was glossy in the light from the oil-lamp and his look when it rested on her was teasing.

'Endeavour?' he asked.

'To try,' she answered.

'I am endeavouring not to tell you how pretty you look,' he grinned.

'Good. Keep trying,' she replied, unable to keep the smile off her face.

'Do you like me?' he asked, still with a teasing glint in his eye.

'Of course,' replied Belinda quickly. 'But——' she stopped.

'But—I think you already have your heart elsewhere?' He smiled again.

'So have you,' she answered. 'At least, so you told me not two days ago.'

'I have,' he replied simply. 'That makes both of us. So now we can be friends.'

Have I got my heart elsewhere? thought Belinda suddenly to herself. It was an unexpected thought and she had answered like that simply because she didn't want any sort of complications, but a troubled look darkened her eyes for a moment. She was beginning to feel that she had got over her crush on Derek. It was easy now to regard him as the father figure in her life, and she knew he too would be relieved at having found a role which would not add complications to his usually well-ordered life. Was it Chuck? Did her heart belong with him? She liked him immensely. Yes, she thought, if her heart was anywhere it was with Chuck. But it was really too early to say anything like that. She slapped down a card triumphantly. 'My game!' They were evenly matched and soon tired of playing. Belinda didn't feel like talking, but she knew some decision about the next few days would have to be made. She had had a good look round and there was simply no way of getting a message back to base. Even if she had wanted to she couldn't have managed to ask Chuck to come out any earlier. They really were stuck here in the wilds with nothing but a long prospect of endless card games to look forward to.

'Tell me honestly, Taqaq, what do you think the chances are of anyone happening to come through this way in the next few days with the news of the Nasaq? It's hardly Piccadilly Circus, is it?' She noted the look of mystification in his eyes. 'What I mean is,' she explained, 'the chances of anyone coming here, anyone we could ask for news about the Nasaq—well,' she sat back with a sigh, 'it's just not very likely, is it?'

Taqaq's frown relaxed a little. 'I tell you my people are a little northwards of here. It's a day's journey. You come with me. They may know something.'

'But what about the rendezvous with Chuck? One day there, one day back—that's cutting it fine,' she countered.

Taqaq shrugged. 'So impatient!' he smiled at her. 'Don't worry, Belinda. Old Sanderson will awaken. He doesn't know what he knows right now. In the morning everything will be different. If not tomorrow, then the day after. Something will happen, I know it. If it's meant to, it will.' He put the cards aside. 'You want me to show you some cats' cradles?' Belinda looked blank. Taking a piece of string from out of his pocket, Taqaq dexterously wove it around his fingers, then held it out to her.

'Oh, I see,' said Belinda, the light dawning. 'We used to do this as children.' She took the string off his hands. Anything to pass the time. An hour later she was grudgingly moved to admiration. It seemed that the patterns Taqaq could make were endless, and he explained that on long dark winter nights, in the snowhouses, the Eskimos would amuse themselves for hours with the ancient string patterns which had been handed down for generations. 'No television, no cinema in the ice-fields,' he explained with a grin. Belinda chuckled. She would have something to tell her colleagues when she got back. She could bet her bottom dollar that none of them would have included cats' cradles in their academic research!

With an eye to the early start necessary the next day if they were to push on to Taqaq's home ground, they decided to call it a night. Taqaq had offered her the choice of sleeping near the stove—and incidentally near Sanderson, who was still snoring like a hog—or the use of the unheated room with the bunk in it. 'In the days of its original glory this would no doubt have been the master bedroom,' said Belinda wryly. She had taken one look at Sanderson, out like a light, and plumped for the spare room.

Taqaq seemed relieved. 'I have the heater and the musical accompaniment,' he grinned. 'Old Sanderson is not going to believe we sleep like this,' he smiled. 'But that's for Sanderson himself to sort out.'

'Let's hope he's sober enough tomorrow to sort something out,' rejoined Belinda, as Taqaq chivalrously carried her things into the spare room and dropped them down by the bunk.

'Not the Ritz,' he said, showing off his grasp of English.

'Where have you heard that phrase?' she asked curiously.

'Your Englishman, Amaruq,' he said, turning to go. 'He teaches us some English conversational gambits sometimes.'

Belinda smiled at the turn of phrase. It had the ironic ring of something Barron might have said himself. 'Why do you call him Amaruq?' she asked, suddenly conscious of her rapidly beating heart as if the answer could possibly have any significance for her.

Taqaq merely shrugged. 'He's like a wolf, no?' he asked, puzzled.

'How? How do you mean?' breathed Belinda.

'Well, he doesn't stop until he has his prey.' Taqaq again turned to go.

'I don't understand.' Belinda wanted to detain him. 'Wait!' She tried to make her voice sound casual. 'I thought names were pretty important. I mean—naming ceremonies are an important part of life here. They signify something important in a person's life, don't they?'

Taqaq looked down at his feet. 'It's what you call a nickname, isn't it?' He half turned, a suspicion of colour flooding his face. 'There are some things no one should ask,' he said at last. With a small smile he made his way back into the main room.

As Belinda unrolled her sleeping bag, she could hear him moving about, then the glow from the oil lamp was quenched and all fell silent—at least, if the occasional grunt from the still flat-out Sanderson and the racket from the gale blowing outside could be discounted. Belinda curled up inside her sleeping bag. She was puzzled by Taqaq's sudden change when she had asked him about Barron, and she felt rather put out at being ticked off. Almost as if she had been treading dangerous ground in some way. What was so special about Barron that the Eskimos could have this almost reverential attitude to him? Or was it something else? Fear, perhaps?

Belinda didn't expect sleep to come quickly, but it was with a shock that she found herself being jerked abruptly awake. It was still dark, but a light seemed to hover above her head. She heard Taqaq's voice coming urgently out of the darkness.

'Is it time to go already?' she asked drowsily. The light dipped.

'We must make the most of the time,' said Taqaq. 'It's a difficult climb at the other end of the valley. Sanderson is talking, but refuses to say anything about the Nasaq. He knows something, but he's being awkward.'

'Damn that man!' cried Belinda, sitting bolt upright. Taqaq took a step back. 'I'm sorry,' she said shortly. It wasn't Sanderson she meant anyway. The smell of bacon and coffee came through the partially open door. She felt suddenly guilty of leaving everything to Taqaq. 'I'll be with you right away,' she said. The light bobbed again and she saw that he had placed it on the floor beside the bunk and had silently left the room. With only the most cursory toilette, Belinda stumbled out to greet the day.

They had been walking steadily for two hours in the direction of the summer camp of the Nasaq, and in all that time it had only been a faint glimmer of light from the horizon that told them day had come.

Belinda had once or twice caught Taqaq's worried glance as he looked at the sky, but when she questioned him he merely shrugged and said they must press on. Another hour or so passed without incident. Belinda's rucksack was beginning to cut into her shoulders and she longed to stop for a rest. Had Derek realised what he was letting her in for? she wondered idly. She doubted it. His feelings weren't such that they would deliberately set out to finish things between them in so brutal a fashion. He had always been thoughtful and considerate. No doubt he would be appalled when she told him what she had had to go through. She was just wondering if she ought to venture the words 'mug-up' when the first flakes of snow began to drift down.

She and Taqaq exchanged brief glances. His expression was difficult to read and Belinda was so surprised by the sight of the drifts of white that she said nothing at first. Perhaps it was just a preliminary fall, a sort of prelude to the big freeze due in a couple of weeks. A seed of anxiety began to grow in her. Surely the weather station hadn't been wrong in its prediction? No, they used the latest satellite communications nowadays and in this part of the world where an inaccurate forecast could mean the difference between life and death, mistakes would surely be a rare event.

Still, after an hour the snow showed no signs of stopping

and was coming down in steady and ever-thickening drifts.
It wasn't long before the ground was covered by a thick
crust of hardening white and the deerskin parkas of the
two figures were soon indistinguishable. It was becoming
increasingly difficult to walk too, as the drifting snow was
being blown by a freshening wind straight off the ground
into their faces. Taqaq moved on a few paces ahead so
that Belinda could follow him and get some protection
from the hard granules that were beginning to bite into
their faces like flying bullets. They proceeded in this way
for a few more hundred yards when suddenly Taqaq
stopped, and half blinded by the snow as she was, Belinda
cannoned into him. He half pushed her down, forcing her
pack off her shoulders and dropping it down next to his
own to form a shield against the drifts. She crouched down
beside him and stared about with large frightened eyes.
Surprisingly he gave her a white-toothed grin and settling
back comfortably with his back against their kit, took out
the bits and pieces with which to roll himself a cigarette.
She watched in mystification as he started to fill the paper
with tobacco.

'What are we going to do?' she cried distractedly. 'We'll
freeze to death if we stay here.'

Taqaq grinned again. Already the blizzard had obliterated any slight landmarks on the route and visibility was
down to a couple of yards. Belinda stood up in a panic
and tried to urge Taqaq to do likewise. She was suddenly
helpless and very frightened, with no guide as to which
direction they should be going. Taqaq dragged her back
into the shelter of the rucksacks. 'That's the white man's
way, to keep on walking, to tire yourself out. That way
you get lost and freeze to death.'

Belinda gaped at him in dismay. 'But what else can we
do?' Her voice became shrill. 'We can't stay here!' All she
could hear was the moaning of the wind and the rattle of
the snow bullets on the frozen leather of her hood.

Taqaq took a deep pull on his cigarette and surveyed

her calmly. 'The Eskimo way is to burrow into a drift and let the snow protect him from the cold.'

Belinda looked sceptical, but she was too frightened by the suddenness of the change to argue. With the snow becoming deeper every minute, she crouched down in the lee of the baggage as Taqaq had told her. 'You are like most white people,' he said. 'You have no patience. Let the snow itself do the job for you. We can sit this storm out. No trouble, no rush.' He grinned again, quite unperturbed by the turn in the weather. 'It's lucky for us old Sanderson was filled to the eyebrows with whisky. It means we are not lacking either.' He produced the bottle Mac had given for Belinda to barter with and unscrewed the lid. Sitting in a snowstorm a hundred miles out in the tundra, with a smiling and unflappable Eskimo and a bottle of whisky, wasn't exactly her idea of fun, nor, come to that, of serious academic research. She groaned inwardly. This was all due to that man and his interference in her plans. She was sure now that he had had some hand in Sanderson's reticence about telling them what he knew. She began to wish fervently that she had a seat in a noisy little aircraft piloted by a pilot with rusty-coloured hair and was heading due south.

The same thought recurred many times in the next twenty-four hours. In that time the blizzard showed no sign of letting up. When it gradually became obvious that they were in for a long wait Taqaq got out the storm tent and fixed it up. Thanks to his know-how they were relatively warm at first in their makeshift shelter and Belinda dozed fitfully, warmed by the whisky and the snug water-proofing of the deerskins. She thanked her lucky stars time and time again that she had discarded the pink quilted number and had not been too vain to forget fashion for a while and dress native-style. In between sleeping and waking Taqaq told her that a storm could last for three or four days in these parts, but when her eyes rounded in horror, he told her not to worry, at this time of year it was highly unlikely that it would go on much longer. She tried to sleep properly, but all her dreams involved a tall, cruel man who was barring her way with a sardonic smile playing around his lips. Whenever she tried to get past him he snarled and revealed large claws that scratched her neck and drew blood. She cried out and came to with a start.

'Bad dreams?' asked Taqaq. 'You must see the shaman.'

Belinda, still half asleep, murmured something about the blizzard going away. Sure enough the wind eventually began to drop, and before long Taqaq suggested that they make their way outside. Snow had built up solidly around them so that they had to crawl on hands and knees through the gap Taqaq had painstakingly kept free through the long hours of their imprisonment.

Outside it was a world transformed. Before the change, nightfall had been of the blackest, but now with the ground covered over in a luminous white mantle the reflected light gave off a radiance that made the dark light. Belinda gazed about with astonished delight. She forgot for a moment the fact that they were miles from the nearest help. Only a distant howling, which faded almost as soon as her hearing picked it out, brought home to her the isolation of their position. She was amazed at first how little affected by the ordeal she was, and felt that it was the new beauty of the magically transformed landscape that was having the most profound effect upon her senses. She turned to Taqaq with a face itself transformed from one creased with anxiety to one of an almost ethereal beauty. He was stopped for a moment by the change. He could not fathom her desire to meet the Nasaq. He thought them a cold and puritanical group of people, unwilling to adapt to change, jealous of their status on the periphery of the Eskimo Nation, but if this girl wanted to meet them, he would move heaven and earth to allow her to do so. He hadn't admitted that he was puzzled too by Sanderson's reluctance to talk about them, but when Belinda made as if to start the long trek back to Sanderson's place he put out a hand to stop her. 'We've come so far,' he told her simply, 'don't give up now. We can make it to the old summer camp of the Nasaq. It's not too far now. We have the choice. Do you feel fit enough to go on?'

'As long as we meet our deadline with Chuck,' she replied.

Taqaq shrugged and glanced briefly at the snow which covered them round in all directions. 'Progress will be slow now,' he told her.

'He stressed how important it was that we should be at our rendezvous on time.'

Taqaq gave a reassuring shake of the head. 'No need to worry. We'll borrow a sled and get back to Sanderson's place in plenty of time. The only difficulty is in getting out to the camp.'

'But can we be sure anyone will be there now?' asked Belinda. She looked doubtful until he reassured her again.

'It's O.K. It's twice as quick to travel by sled. Very speedy. No problem.'

Belinda was more than half convinced. She felt she had to be after coming all this way. Anything must be quicker than travelling over this pathless waste on foot. 'I'm game to go on,' she said with a spark of determination.

'Come on,' urged Taqaq, shouldering his pack. He set off before she could protest, and she was forced to follow at a run until she caught up. She had a feeling of light-headedness now, and put it down to the whisky and the fitful night's sleep in the cramped little tent, but there was no time to muse on her physical state. They walked at a brisk pace and Belinda found she needed to put all her attention into keeping her balance. It wasn't easy walking over the hard-packed ice. The snow had frozen to a shell with soft loose snow in a thin covering on top.

For an hour or more nothing could be heard but the
squeak of their boots and their own laboured breathing.

Belinda knew Taqaq was driving her hard, and the
thought gave her a feeling of unease. His words had
sounded confident and he had shown no expression of
disquiet, yet whenever she had tried to slow down he had
urged her forward mercilessly. Eventually she was forced
to ask him what was so urgent. 'It's already night,' she
said, looking at the moon scudding icily between thick
banks of cloud, 'why can't we take our time? Why can't
we stop to have something to eat? Can't we even have a
mug-up? I'm starving! I could eat a bear!'

Taqaq looked at her strangely. 'Nannuq?' His face was
impassive.

'Look here,' cried Belinda, 'don't just walk on. Answer
me.'

Taqaq stopped just where he was. 'It is best to put our
best foot forward,' he said in precise English. 'Are you
tired?'

'No, just hungry and thirsty,' replied Belinda a trifle
weepily. 'You seem to be able to go for ages without food,
Taqaq. How on earth do you do it?'

Taqaq came back to where she was standing. He could
see every detail of her lovely face in the moonlight as if it
had been as light as day. He could understand the young
pilot's possessiveness. Chuck had made no bones about
what he would do if anything happened to Belinda. Now,
because of the vulnerability her face expressed, he knew
there were things he could not tell her. Distantly the
blood-freezing sound of a wolf broke the stillness. 'Keep
on the move,' he urged, wondering if she recognised the
sound. 'Another hour, not much more.'

Belinda heaved a tired sigh. The cold seemed to eat
into her very bones. She eased her shoulders beneath the
straps and, following Taqaq's lead, once again began to
stumble after him. At least they were still on the trail, she
thought, at least there was still a sporting chance of

success. If things worked out, she would eventually get her way. She *would* make contact with Barron's friends. She *would* show him she couldn't be beaten.

They walked a long way, it seemed to her, though their progress was difficult. After a time she simply gave herself up to the rhythm of their footsteps. There was no point trying to think where they were going. She had become unaware of the cold which earlier had kept her teeth chattering and had begun to crack her lips. Now it was simply a question of trudging on over the flat white plain.

She came to with a jolt. The first thing she noticed was the silence now that their footsteps were stopped. It was as if she had been walking in her sleep. Taqaq was standing a couple of paces in front of her. He was quite motionless. He looked like a figure carved in snow with his head on one side, listening for something in the still night air. The moon had gone behind some cloud now and the sky was quite overcast. But the lightness of the snow gave a kind of half light and anything on its surface stood out in stark relief. Belinda allowed her eyes to follow the direction of Taqaq's gaze where his eyes raked the distant plain. Suddenly she stiffened. Far away across the snow there was the unmistakable sign of something moving towards them. Even as she watched, she could see that it was slowly getting closer. Taqaq was motionless as if turned to ice. Belinda strained her ears. Very faintly, with a sort of blood-chilling distance to it, came the thin yapping of several dogs. She watched cautiously, scarcely daring to breathe, the sound still so faint in its rise and fall that it was easy to feel mistaken. But the shape came closer so that Belinda gradually began to be able to make out that it was not one but several shapes, in fact it was a whole pack of dogs running rapidly and closely together over the snows towards them. The blood froze in her veins as she heard the eerie howl of the lead dog rise up above the broken yelps of the rest of the pack. Icy fingers played up and down her spine. For a moment she dared not speak. When the words finally came, it was simply to breathe Taqaq's name. She moved up alongside him, her breath shallow with fear. Convulsively her fingers gripped his arm. 'What is it, Taqaq?' she whispered, half dead with fright.

He turned to her, his face impassive, eyes, as ever, calm and dark and giving nothing away. He said one word: 'Amaruq.'

Belinda's heart missed a beat. Her blood froze. 'Wolves?' The pack were leaping and barking, by now no more than five hundred yards away and getting closer every second. A little cry forced itself from between her parted lips, then she felt herself falling, falling into the cold blackness of oblivion.

CHAPTER SEVEN

WHEN she came to the first thing she noticed was a sort of bumping, swaying motion. For a moment she lay back with her eyes closed. She imagined she must be back home somewhere, or on a train, or a plane, perhaps, but there was no roar of the engine, no sound at all, except a rushing whoosh, like skis over snow. In her fuddled state she fancied she must be skiing, but no, that was nonsense. She was lying down, and lying down on something distinctly furry. She forced her eyes open. Overhead were tiny pinpricks of a thousand stars. There was nothing to show that she was moving along except for the bumping and jolting that rocked her from side to side. Distantly she was able to make out the sound of dogs, and with a sudden rush of memory the picture came flooding back. Panic-stricken, she tried to sit up, but a lurch in the conveyance threw her sideways and for a moment she lay where she had been thrown. After a moment's rest she made one more try and managed to struggle up on to one elbow. No wonder she was warm! A huge bearskin covered her, wrapping her limbs tightly and making it difficult to move.

Desperate now to find out where she was, she managed to keep her balance long enough to have a look round. With a shock of surprise she saw that she was on a large sled. It was being pulled along at quite a pace by a team of a dozen or so huskies. The soft swooshing sound that had reminded her of skis was the sound of the runners over the ice. It was very soothing. She flopped down again, surprised at the heaviness of her limbs, but in a moment she was raising her head yet again. So far she hadn't been able to see who was driving the sleigh, but when she managed to edge herself round a little, she found she could lift the flap of her hood and take a peep from beneath it. Taqaq was sitting on the board behind her, a passenger, it seemed, like herself. He noticed at once that she was awake and she saw the brief flash of his teeth as he smiled down at her. The driver was standing up on the transom behind him, a long whip flicking expertly over the backs of the dogs in front, and Taqaq called out something in Eskimo to him.

Belinda relaxed back among the furs. So they were safe. The dreadful nightmare about the pack of wolves had been just that, a dream and no more. She gave a shuddering sigh of relief. Obviously some of Taqaq's relatives had come out to meet them and this was the sled transport he had promised. It was certainly fast! The driver was forcing the team on at a terrific pace. They would soon be in the camp and she would be able to start work on her assignment at last. She hugged herself with excitement. She was going to do it! At last she was going to do it—despite the opposition. It was certainly a turn-up for the books getting a lift in what looked like a desolate waste land. Mac had told her that whole families lived out here, seeking a living from the land, but after yesterday's blizzard she found it hard to believe that there was a living soul within a thousand miles. She lay back contentedly.

It wasn't many minutes before the driver was giving a guttural cry of command to the dogs and the sled began to slow. In another moment it had come to a skidding full stop and the driver was getting down. Belinda once more struggled into a sitting position, still puzzled by the strange heaviness in her limbs.

There were no particular landmarks in sight. They seemed to be still in the middle of nowhere. I expect the camp is over the brow of a hill, she thought. She pulled her hood a little closer. The wind was as penetrating as ever. Now, however, there was no falling snow to contend with.

Taqaq said something to the driver and got up off the sled. Belinda watched the two men walk a little way into the snow. One of them bent down and she saw that he held a kind of stick in his hand which he thrust deep into the banked snowdrifts. The other man said something and the taller of the two stood up.

The thought flicked into Belinda's mind that there was something familiar about the man with the stick, but after her previous night of slightly delirious dreams she put it down to a mild recurrence of the same thing. Then the man turned and walked straight back towards her. The long fur of his hood partially obscured his face and it was still dark, but there was no mistaking the set of those broad shoulders, the easy athletic movement of the limbs, as he made his way over the ice towards the sled.

The icy hand of fear clutched her heart. It must be a bad dream!

Belinda watched fascinated as he approached, not wanting to believe the evidence of her own eyes. There was no way it could be him. Not here. She was having another bad dream. She would have pinched herself to make sure she was awake if he hadn't come right up to the sled. Then there was no mistaking the reality of the situation. He threw down the snow stick so that it clattered against the wooden board on which she was lying, then without taking any notice of her he walked round to the front of the sled where he began to unfasten the harnessing of the dogs. Still without speaking to her, but very definitely no figment of the imagination, he led the brutes away from the sled. Leaping and yapping around his legs, they were tied to a stake and he started to throw some hunks of meat to them. That quietened them down and, still without even looking at her, he came back to the sled. When Taqaq made his way back too Belinda was still sitting, half lying, speechless, not quite believing her eyes. She watched him take a knife from the bundle of equipment before rousing herself enough to call his name.

'Taqaq!' she called.

'O.K. now?' he asked with concern showing briefly in his face. She looked askance at him.

'What's that man doing here?' she asked, not even trying to keep the note of dismay out of her voice. Taqaq looked back to where Barron had gone back to busy himself with the dogs.

'Amaruq?' he grinned. 'Lucky for us, eh?' He reached down and freed the knife from its fastening, then with no more word of explanation he made his way to the place where Barron had plunged in the snowstick and started to hack at the ice. Belinda lay back with a sense of defeat. Would this man stop at nothing in his determination to prevent her meeting with the Nasaq? Why was it so important to him? She pulled herself bolt upright. She still felt vaguely groggy. Everything seemed swimmy as if it was all taking place at a distance. She felt no need for constraint or pretence now. This was open war. Her anger made her call out peremptorily to Barron, using his English name.

He heard her. He must have heard her, she noted irritably, but he didn't at once lift his head. It seemed to

Belinda that he was deliberately taking his time over his chore with the dogs, and she stifled a cry of irritation.

This time she would not lose her temper. But she would find out just what he thought he was doing here—what right he thought he had to interfere with her work, driving up out of nowhere with his rabble of half-wild mongrels, scaring her half to death so that she actually passed out in the snow.

She paused, bothered by this.

It was the first time she had ever fainted in her life. She called out again, and started to get out from beneath the piled-up skins. Barron turned then and loped swiftly over to her. His face was unsmiling as he approached. There were no words of greeting on his lips. Belinda stifled a memory of how they had felt on her own, and a flicker of resentment showed in her face. 'You!' she said. He stood, unspeaking, by the side of the sled. 'Would you mind telling me what's happening?'

'Do you want something?' was his reply.

'I want to know what's happening,' she repeated. 'Why you of all people? Where have you brought me? What are you doing? Why have you unhitched the dogs? And what is Taqaq doing?'

'Steady on!' he said, lifting one of the skins back to tuck it in round her legs.

'Don't do that!' she almost shouted, pushing the skin off again. 'What do you think I am, an invalid or something? I demand to know what's going on!'

Barron gave her an ill-concealed look of something like contempt and began to walk away. Belinda at once swung her legs down off the sled, letting the skins fall any old how on the snow. She took a step forward, determined to make him stop and give some account of himself, but suddenly, as if from nowhere, the snow seemed to come up and hit her hard in the face. The next thing she knew she was being bundled up in the furs again and strong arms were holding her struggling ones still. She was dumped unceremoniously back on to the sled. When she opened her eyes she was looking into the disturbingly blue ones of Barron. His face was too close for comfort. She tried to struggle free, but he held her tight and she could feel the warmth of his skin on her cheek. With a little twist she managed to turn her face away, but her hood slipped back and she felt his face pressing into her hair. 'What on earth are you doing?' she shouted, twisting and turning angrily.

'I'm trying to get some silly girl back on to the sled where I put her in the first place. And,' he paused dangerously, 'if she doesn't stop being such a flaming nuisance she'll have to have a good hiding like any other misbehaving animal!'

'I'm not the one who's misbehaving!' she flared. 'Get your hands off me! You—you——'

'Desperado?' he offered drily. 'Barbarian?'

'It's better than carrion or commodity anyway,' Belinda whipped back.

'So that's what's bugging you,' he smiled easily. 'Rash words in the heat of anger. Don't you ever forgive and forget?'

'Not when you meant every word of it,' she replied, suddenly weakening beneath the amused glint in his eyes. 'Anyway, you still haven't answered any of my questions. And I don't see why I should do as you say. Who do you think you are?'

'I thought you knew that,' he said amusedly, ignoring the first part of what she'd said. 'I'm Amaruq.'

She gave a short laugh of derision. 'Of course! Still playing at Eskimos,' she retorted. 'I'd forgotten.'

His face looked stern. 'Don't for one minute think this is anything like a game.' His eyes had taken on the hard look she had seen earlier. He gripped her by the shoulders. 'This is no game.' She shivered as he repeated the words with more intensity. 'Stay where I put you.' He pushed her back among the furs, and she felt too weak to resist.

For a moment his glance held hers, then he reached into a bag and brought out a bottle of something. She couldn't see what it was, but he forced it against her lips as if to make her drink from it.

'I won't! I won't!' she cried, twisting and turning again. 'I won't be made to drink. I won't!'

'Please yourself,' he said easily, putting the bottle to his own lips. He drank deeply, then went over to Taqaq and offered the bottle to him. Taqaq drank, wiped the neck and handed it back. Lazily Barron came back to the sled and put one foot on the outer edge. He thrust the bottle into Belinda's hands. 'I don't know what you're bothered about. Do you think I'm going to drug you and then rape you? It's only a fruit syrup.'

His look told her he thought she was a stiffnecked little fool. She felt suddenly small and weak and very helpless, and to her dismay, tears began to form in the corners of her eyes. She tried to turn her head away so that he wouldn't see them, but he was too sharp for tricks like that. 'What's the matter?' He peered closely into her face. 'Aren't you feeling better?'

'I'm all right,' she said in a small voice. 'There's nothing the matter with me. It's just—it's——'

'Yes?' he urged, and she looked up. Barron's face seemed momentarily full of concern. A trick of the light, she thought drily with a flash of her old spirit. 'What's the matter now?' he asked more brusquely.

'I'm sick and tired of being bullied by you,' she said in a tight little voice. 'Everywhere I go, you seem to be there, laying down the law, telling me what to do, telling me what to think, trying to stop me from doing my job.'

'Don't you think you're exaggerating all this a bit?' he asked.

'No, I don't!' she exploded, blinking the tears away. 'Who told Sanderson not to help me?' She paused, her eyes searching his face angrily. When he didn't reply she went on: 'Here I am, miles from anywhere, and who should come pounding over the snows with a team of highly dangerous and no doubt rabid dogs but you! It's impossible!'

'That team of possibly rabid dogs,' he broke in drily, 'has also possibly saved your life.' And before she could explode in disbelief, he went on, 'And if you will set out on these ill-planned and ridiculous expeditions, you can expect more than just me and my dogs to come to the rescue. Tomorrow at first light I can guarantee at least one plane from the R.C.M.P.' He looked down at her sternly, his hands thrust under his armpits in an attempt to keep them warm, his eyes for once serious.

'The R.C.M.P.?' repeated Belinda weakly. She had a brief vision of a horde of red-coated Mounties in broad-brimmed stetsons, galloping to the rescue over the distant horizon. She let an uncontrollable giggle escape her. It owed more to fear and weakness than amusement, but she leaned back anyway, tears of another sort crowding her eyes.

'Blow me, what's up now?' demanded Barron roughly. 'First you pass out at the sight of me and my dogs, next you——'

She stiffened. 'Don't flatter yourself! How was I to know it was only you?' she demanded scornfully. 'I thought it was a pack of wolves bearing down on us. All Taqaq said when I asked him what it was, was "Amaruq"—what else would any normal person be expected to think in the circumstances?' She looked at him through glistening lashes.

'It depends on the context that a normal person would find themselves in,' he replied patronisingly. His even white teeth revealed themselves briefly in a smile. 'I'm sorry I frightened you, though. I thought you'd passed out in the excitement of seeing me.'

'Ha!' Her laugh was full of scorn.

'You're far too changeable for your own good, you know,' he looked serious for a moment. 'Now tell me something, are you going to do as you're told and stay wrapped up till we've finished?'

'Finished what?' she demanded. Barron gestured towards Taqaq. Already he had made several blocks from the hard-packed snow and had built them into the beginnings of a wall. 'What's he doing?' Belinda asked cautiously.

'It'll be a snow house. Sorry about this—it looks as if you've got to go native for a couple of days.' He made as if to go.

'What did you say?' she demanded, jerking herself upright again. Barron walked away, deliberately, with only a brief backward glance. She half rose, intending to go after him, but remembering what had happened last time, she paused. He was quick to notice anything she did and turned round as if guessing her intention. 'Anyone who gets off that sled without my permission gets a hiding,' he warned. 'It works for dogs, there's no reason why such treatment shouldn't work for disobedient humans too.'

An uncontrollable fury rose in Belinda, and her fists bunched helplessly in their mittens. 'I hate you!' she stormed. 'I think you're the most ill-bred, arrogant, presumptuous man I've ever met!' She pounded the side of the sled with her fists. All Barron did was burst into peals of laughter, and with his own long snow knife he joined Taqaq in cutting out more blocks of ice for for the snow house.

Despite her fury, Belinda felt vaguely relieved that she was not expected to muck in. It was true she felt weak and slightly dizzy. Waves of cold kept making her teeth chatter despite the furs and she wondered if perhaps she had hit her head on something the first time she fell. It was so unlike her to be ill that she tried to brace up, and surreptitiously took a drink or two from the bottle of fruit syrup. But it did no immediate good, and she turned her back on the two men and pretended to sleep.

Perhaps sleep did steal over her, for when she next came

round, she could hear the two men talking quietly somewhere close at hand, so that when she turned over to have
a look at them she was met by the sight of the completed
house. It was only small, but the men must have worked
hard to finish it. Belinda lay resigned where she was. Still
weak, she was beginning to think that she had better do
as Barron said, because if she didn't she had no doubt
that he would carry out his threat to chastise her. He has
no respect for anyone or anything, she thought bitterly.
It's a good job Taqaq is here. At least I can rely on him
to see that Barron doesn't overstep the mark. Noticing
some movement from the sled, the two men came over.

'You can get down now,' said Barron, switching into
English. 'Can you walk?'

'Of course I can walk,' replied Belinda in surprise. 'Why
shouldn't I be able to?'

'You were a little dizzy last time,' he replied casually.
'It's usual in cases of hypothermia.' He made as if to help
her.

'Wait a moment,' she broke in. 'Hypothermia?'

'You're not tough enough to spend so long out in a
blizzard,' he said. 'Your body hasn't yet adapted to the
cold. It's Taqaq's guess I came across you just in time.'
He put an arm under her shoulders and shushing her
flood of protestations, lifted her easily and carried her
towards the snow house.

'I don't know what you're talking about, but I hope
you'll explain soon,' she said.

Barron tightened his grip for a moment. 'Wait until we
get inside. You always need to know the whys and wherefores at once,' he told her critically.

'Naturally,' she retorted with as much spirit as she could
muster, 'because there are such a lot of unexplained whys
and wherefores whenever you seem to be around.' She
stopped talking long enough to crawl in through the
entrance as he instructed, then she turned to him expectantly. He shushed her again and made her wrap up in

the furs from off the sled. Then he lit a small heater and
set up the stone lamp to one side so that his face was
illuminated fully in its steady glow. Gone was his sneering
look of previous meetings and when he turned the full
gaze of his blue eyes on her Belinda was struck by an
unaccustomed look of something like gentleness in their
depths. She shivered as he eased his muscular body into a
sitting position and when he was comfortable he returned
her glance with some amusement. 'I guess you have a
right to a few questions,' he told her, 'whether you have a
right to any answers remains to be seen.' Belinda bit off
the words of protest that naturally sprang to her lips and
instead managed a wan smile.

'Tell me about the hypothermia first,' she asked in a
small voice.

'When the temperature of the body core drops below a
certain level a feeling of lassitude and lightheadedness
ensues,' he replied authoritatively. 'If steps are not taken
immediately to bring the temperature up to normal again,
eventually death will follow. Recognise any of the symp-
toms?' he demanded.

Belinda gave an involuntary shudder. 'But I didn't feel
cold once we started walking,' she said. 'It wore off.'

'Precisely,' he said. 'That's one of the dangers. Once
thoroughly chilled, the body no longer responds in the
normal way.'

'I have been feeling rotten, sort of heavy and sleepy——'
Her teeth still chattered uncontrollably every few minutes.
'I suppose I have to thank you, then,' she spoke quietly.
'It was lucky you turned up. Or was it only luck?' She
waited expecting some sort of explanation, but instead
he looked serious.

'You certainly gave Taqaq a fright,' he told her. 'He
thought you were coping all right until you suddenly
passed out. He had the fright of his life. He said he's not
used to people keeling over without any warning. When I
saw what had happened I gave him a bawling out as

well. Good job he's an equable sort of bloke. You ought to say something to him,' he added on a more sombre note, 'he's feeling bad about it.'

'I will, I will,' she nodded eagerly. 'He's been nothing but kindness to me.'

Barron looked mockingly at her. 'Does that surprise you?' he asked. 'I would have thought you were quite used to people, especially men, being kind, as you put it——' and before she could deny it, he added, 'Maybe that's why you're such a spoilt brat and need to be taken in hand.'

Colour rose hotly to her cheeks. 'That's not fair——' she began at once, but Barron lifted his hand.

'Listen!' he said. Outside they could hear the sudden racket of the dogs starting up their howling. Then, as suddenly, they fell silent. Far off came a single lone howl. It sounded several miles away, but the howling echoed back and forth in the still, cold air, and immediately the dogs joined in. It was eerie to hear the dogs howl at different, spaced-out intervals, and yet after they all got going again, they stopped, all of them, instantly. It was a sound that lifted the hairs on Belinda's head, and she shivered with more than just cold, and looked in alarm at Barron. His eyes were soft with some emotion she could not name. 'It's the symphony of the Arctic,' he told her.

For a moment neither of them spoke. Belinda was stirred by a surge of unexpected emotion. She let out a long slow breath. Somehow, bit by bit, her fear of Barron was beginning to recede. She felt his glance rest on her for a moment, and slowly she raised her face towards his. The stone lamp gave a warm, glowing luminosity to her delicate skin so that for a moment Barron simply looked long and slowly at her as if drinking in every detail of her features. Then he leaned forward and slowly pushed her hood back without speaking so that her hair came tumbling free in a golden fall of curls. She felt his fingers for a moment, deep in the thickness of her hair, and im-

mediately and unbidden came the recollection of that time
at the settlement when he had plunged his hands into the
thick coat of the dog he was buying. Swiftly on the heels
of that memory came the sequel and the repugnance she
had felt. It broke the spell at once, and she jerked her
head back. Her face hardened and she averted her glance.
Barron stiffened as if she had actually spoken her feelings
and when she risked a glance at him, his eyes had regained
the hard shuttered look she had seen so many times
before.

'Well,' she said, drawing the furs tightly round her
knees, 'you still haven't told me how it is that you've
managed to appear so propitiously out of the blue?' She
regarded him defiantly. He made a movement as if to get
up and his reply was curt.

'I was out setting traplines.'

'But you were in the settlement when I left, how on
earth did you get up here so quickly?'

'There are ways,' he replied unhelpfully. When she
waited for him to continue he said, 'Some routes are unsuitable for greenhorns like you. Especially ones carrying
a lot of expensive recording equipment. Personally I've
always found it best to travel light.'

'Yes,' she said drily, 'I'd noticed.' She hesitated.

'Any more questions?'

He looked bored. There was a coldness between them
now. Belinda couldn't help remembering Ikluk, the cry of
greeting, the conversation outside the house, the things
Mac had told her about native marriage customs. There
were certainly more questions. Instead she only said,
'Questions without answers, perhaps.' She hesitated. 'I
suppose you'll tell me why you said I'd have to go native
for a couple of days. I mean——' she looked round the
snow house, 'you surely don't intend that three people
should stay in this place for long. I've had rather enough
of Arctic wastes at the moment. I have a rendezvous with
a plane from the private charter company soon.' She

furrowed her brow. Was it tomorrow or the day after? Her sense of time was all to pot. She looked helplessly at Barron, but he was already speaking.

'They might send out a rescue plane too,' he said. 'I think you can forget your rendezvous with Robinson. Eager though he may be to play the hero, they're not likely to let him try to make a landing here—they'd need a snow-plane. Instead they'll simply get on to the rescue service.'

Belinda had a strange sensation when he said that, as if some vital lifeline had been severed. She hadn't realised what her link with the outside world, through the expected meeting with Chuck, had become. Barron's next words only added to her feeling of helplessness.

'When they see we're holed up safe and snug here, they'll fly off again.' She waited for him to go on, but he merely sat on the edge of the sleeping platform, indifferent and remote, waiting for her next question.

'They'll surely try to rescue us——' her words tailed off. Obviously from the air they would imagine everything was all right, that they were coping with the situation, that they needed no help. 'The three days, then,' she persisted, 'what did you mean by that? Why can't we go back to Sanderson's place——' She trailed off, realising that in the face of his impassive response her voice had taken on a rising note of panic. 'You can't keep me here against my will. I want to tell them to take me back to—if we don't let them know, how can we be rescued at all?'

'I don't need to be rescued,' was the laconic reply. 'I'm out earning my keep. I have lines to set. If I don't work I don't eat. I'm not intending to go back to the trading post till I have my quota of silver fox pelts.'

Belinda stared at him in horror. 'What about me?' she whispered. She had a dark and forbidding vision of the long journey back through the ice and snow to the settlement, both of them, Taqaq and herself, struggling on by foot through the treacherous snow. Her feeling of weakness brought tears to her eyes. 'You're playing cat and mouse with me,' she broke out angrily. 'You've got something planned. Why are you holding out on me?' She looked at him with a face flushed with anger. 'I don't want to spend days on end in this little place. Besides, there isn't room for three people.' The thought of spending so much time in such proximity to Barron brought prickles running up and down her spine.

'There won't be three,' he replied quietly. 'Only two.'

'You mean you're abandoning us, while you go off and kill foxes? Well, that's something,' she retorted.

'I don't mean that at all,' he said carefully. 'I can delay my work for a day or two. I'm not the one who's leaving.'

Belinda stared at him. 'What do you mean? I can't——' she froze. A dreadful thought struck her. 'You mean——' she whispered the name, 'Taqaq? He's leaving?' She paused with a sudden frightened glance at the man beside her. 'He's not—he's not leaving me alone——?'

'No,' broke in Barron easily, 'I shall be here. You won't be alone.'

Belinda's hand flew to her mouth.

'You're not fit to travel just yet.'

'Who says?' she demanded, her voice high with emotion.

He merely shrugged his shoulders. Belinda swallowed. She would have a word with Taqaq at once. She would beg him to stay. She would plead with him. She knew he would stay if she asked him to.

'He must have told you he has relatives round here. We thought it would be a good idea if he took the sled and made his way to their camp as quickly as possible. He's very keen to see someone there, I imagine. It's a small camp some miles east of here. He'll be able to get word to the R.C.M.P. that you're safe, so that your friends back at Two Rivers don't start worrying.'

'But I'm not safe!' burst out Belinda. 'Not at all safe—

I'm——' She broke off confusedly.

Barron was smiling strangely. 'Perhaps you're not,' he said simply. 'Perhaps you're in the worst danger imaginable—here, alone with me, a hundred miles from civilisation. Anything could happen. I could kill you after practising unspeakable tortures on your body. No one would ever know.'

Belinda gave him a sharp glance. She knew he was laughing at her, but the knowledge that what he said had a grain of truth in it made her stiffen warily.

'I'm being pleasant now,' he told her with a narrow smile, 'but wait until Taqaq goes. Then I'll reveal my true colours.' He smiled lazily and put out a hand to touch the line of her cheek with the back of one of his fingers. She jerked her head away, drawing her lips back with a cry, and he laughed softly. 'I do like them with a bit of fight. It makes the victory so much more worthwhile.'

Belinda drew up her knees and gave him a steady, unblinking gaze that did nothing to control the beating of her heart. She would not let him see how her blood was racing violently round her body bringing a flush of unwelcome heat with it. She would be calm and aloof, she decided. No matter how or why Barron had cooked up this arrangement with Taqaq, she would not let him see that she was rattled by it. She would have a quiet word with Taqaq as soon as possible. 'When does he leave?' she asked, her thoughts racing.

'Round about now, I should think,' was Barron's reply.

Belinda's heart gave an extra leap. 'I must see him.' She half rose. 'You said I should say something about my blacking out. That it wasn't his fault,' she said, stumbling close to him in her desire to get outside.

'Wait,' he said, rising quickly to his feet. 'You're still in no fit state to go outside. Stay in the warmth. I'll call him.' He stopped and looked down at her, and Belinda felt suddenly faint. He was so tall, so fit and full of vital

good health, and he moved, even in this confined space,
with the ease and grace of a wild animal. Her knees were
turning to jelly and she felt everything swimming round
her.

'Look, you're still not well.' He pushed her gently back
among the furs. For a moment he supported her against
his arm. 'When you looked so distraught at the idea of
not making it in time back to base I nearly suggested that
you go with Taqaq in the sled. But it would be too much
for you. I don't think I realised just how hard you've
been pushing yourself.' He moved his arm away and looked
down at her coldly. 'Try not to be such a nuisance. You're
only making it difficult for both of us.'

Belinda stared miserably as he pushed his way outside.
She could hear the murmur of his voice as he spoke to
Taqaq. In a moment Taqaq poked his head into the snow
house. 'O.K.?' he asked cheerfully. Belinda nodded
warmly. 'Not long and you'll be fighting fit again.' He
gestured over his shoulder. 'More blizzard coming up.
This is the best place for you. I'll tell them in a couple of
days when I get to my people's hunting ground. It's easy
for the snow-plane to land. Here it would be dangerous.
The drifts are too deep. A message will go through to the
trading post.' He raised a hand in some sort of farewell.

'Wait! You can't leave me alone with that man.' She
half rose.

'You'll be safer here,' he told her. 'No bear.'

'Must you go?' she asked him weakly.

'Yes. This is the best plan. Lucky for us Amaruq got
worried. He guessed we'd come out this way from
Sanderson's place. Very lucky.' With that Taqaq was
gone.

Belinda closed her eyes. She could hear the dogs yapping excitedly in their traces, then the sound moved round
the snow house and began to recede. Soon it was just a
faint and distant mingling of howls across the emptiness.
When Barron came in, she let her eyelids remain closed.

She had had a thought which brought another wave of unease down, but it was no good bringing it into the open. It was just that Taqaq's parting words had seemed to suggest that Amaruq really had known all along where the Nasaq were encamped. Her suspicions about who it was who had silenced Sanderson, though drawing a blank when she had queried Barron himself, were in fact correct. He had known all along.

She frowned with anger. His attempt to prevent her meeting them seemed to be more than just sheer bloody-mindedness. It was deliberate obstruction. He had even told Mac that they were hunting outside the region altogether. Now he had more or less kidnapped her, dismissed her guide, and was holding her here, a prisoner in the middle of nowhere. All in an attempt to stop her making a few recordings! It seemed now that the chances of her ever meeting up with the Nasaq, or fulfilling her assignment for Derek, were remote in the extreme. It looked as if finally he would get his way. Unless . . . unless she could escape? She knew it was hopeless. Even if she had been one hundred per cent fit, she would never know where to start, let alone face the long trek to the camp.

Another disturbing thought puckered her brow. What plans did Barron have for her now he had got her prisoner? What had he in mind, now that she was totally in his power? She lay back in the warm furs, limbs rigid with apprehension. She knew that she would have to play it cool, really cool this time, and avoid any possibility of rousing him to anger. She decided that the best course would be to preserve an almost total silence. She wouldn't speak unless it was absolutely necessary. That way he would soon get the message that she was unwilling to be a party to his games. She had no idea how long he intended to keep her prisoner here, but he would find she did not take kindly to this sort of treatment.

As soon as she heard the sound of his returning footsteps, she turned her back and covered her face. She would pretend to be asleep. Undisturbed like that she could work out a strategy for survival. A feeling of desolation over-whelmed her. How far away Derek and her other univer-sity colleagues seemed now. How helpless she was in the territory of this man, this Amaruq—wolf, so-called.

It was the fitful glow of light through the sides of the snow house that woke Belinda late in the afternoon of the next day. The feeling of unreality which had apparently been a symptom of her illness had now disappeared, and the minute she woke she sat up and looked sharply round. Of Barron there was no sign. His sleeping bag was spread out on the platform on the opposite side of the snow house, and seeing it suddenly like that, rumpled, just as he had climbed out of it, sent a little shudder through her. Such proximity to a man who was almost a complete stranger seemed almost indecent, and she wondered if knowing glances would be exchanged if she bothered to mention this part of her adventures to her colleagues back home.

She was just beginning to wonder where Barron had gone to when she heard the sound of someone approach-ing. Involuntarily she put up a hand to try to pat her hair into place – but she needn't have bothered. Barron came straight in with only the most cursory glance in her direction. He crouched down next to the stove, lit it, placed a kettle full of snow on it, then from out of a sort of game bag worn over his shoulder, produced something from it which he proceeded to place in the cooking kettle. Belinda watched, trying to conceal her interest. He seemed quite oblivious to her presence. She found it an ideal opportunity to give him a closer scrutiny than before.

There was, she decided, something commanding in his demeanour, despite his wild hair, which shone with clean-liness and good health. She smiled wryly. He was cer-tainly good-looking, she decided. His knowledge of his physical presence must surely be a contributing factor in his arrogant and high-handed attitude towards her. A man like that must be used to having his own way with women. For him to find one who wouldn't kow-tow to his vanity must be a disturbing experience.

Being with Barron in such intimate circumstances, Belinda couldn't help speculating on his previous experience with women. She became irritable when she pictured the small, dark-haired Ikluk, with the solemn dark eyes and the sweet face of a child. How could such a girl fail to melt the heart of even this man, or if not melt his heart exactly, arouse in him some urge to dominate and impress on her a knowledge of his power and urgency.

There was something sensuous about lying amidst the luxury of fur and leather, and she found she was beginning to drift into a sort of dreaming state somewhere between sleeping and waking. The next hour passed by in this sort of way, but she was abruptly dragged out of this mood by a rough shake on the shoulder. Barron hovered over her with an enamel bowl full of a kind of stew. He offered it without a word and she took it with no word of thanks. It was some sort of partially cooked meat, not, she found to her surprise, particularly unpleasant. He watched her eat with one sardonically raised eyebrow and a half-smile playing round his lips.

'At least I can rustle up a meal from nothing,' he said tauntingly. 'Do you like it?'

Belinda merely gave a half-nod of acceptance, but it seemed to be enough, because he laughed and when she had finished he took her bowl, cleared everything away, and came to sit down on the edge of the sleeping platform beside her. Already the light outside had faded, but he made no move to light the lamp. She could just make out the sharp outline of his jaw when he turned his head away, but his eyes were lost in the shadowed sockets beneath the raven wing of his brow.

'The laconic lady linguist,' he said, settling more comfortably beside her. A little shiver ran through her at the nearness of him. Her breath seemed to catch at the sheer attractiveness of him. She trembled, waiting for him to speak. Instead he merely sat very still, eyes half closed, oblivious to her presence yet again. She let her eyes linger over his shadowed face, then a sudden thought took hold of her. For a moment it made her shudder inwardly. Why was it, she asked herself, that she felt such powerful extremes of emotion when Barron came close to her? Was it love? Could it be love when she felt such anger almost bordering on hatred whenever she felt the whiplash of his biting disapproval? Or was this palpable emotion he aroused so easily in her nothing more than the desire of the flesh? It was desire, yes—a dangerous desire. His savage, almost brutal way of life mixed so strangely with the tenderness and concern he had seemed to show when she was ill. It aroused in her painful sensations which she had never before experienced.

Barron was looking at her closely now as if for signs of further delirium. Belinda wondered what he would say if she revealed her thoughts to him. Laugh derisively, perhaps. Take advantage of the situation, most certainly. Add her to his list of exchange partners, no doubt. When he did finally speak her nerves were already strung up enough to make any answer predictably sharp. She scarcely heard what he said. The words that immediately sprang to her own lips were, 'Don't bother. I don't want any more favours.' Then she could have bitten her tongue off when she realised what he had been saying. His words had been the very words she had wanted to hear ever since arriving at the settlement. He had said: 'Tomorrow I've arranged for you to meet the Nasaq. I'll translate for you if you like.'

Now she stared in dismay at the change in his expression. Her own thoughts were in turmoil. Was this some new gambit in his game of chess with her? What sort of promise was it? Was he hoping to gain her gratitude by making such a promise? She watched in silent misery as he brusquely rose to his feet and moved towards the door.

'I didn't mean—I——' she paused. When Barron looked at her with such depths of coldness in his eyes she found it impossible to frame the words of apology that could heal this fresh wound in their relationship. The trouble was, she felt she could not trust herself.

He looked down at her for a moment, his lips curling in a savage smile.

'Quite the response I would have expected from the ice maiden,' he said, and Belinda bit her lip.

'That's not fair,' she said in a low voice.

He gave her a look of contempt and started to unroll his sleeping bag. She watched miserably. She was certainly fooling herself if she imagined she had hurt his feelings by her sharp reply. Despite the look which had briefly shadowed his face his every movement now expressed contempt for her.

Of course, she was just an inconvenience to him. His manner gave her no room to doubt that. He had Ikluk and perhaps other partners. It was his misfortune, his manner seemed to tell her, that he was stuck with her for the next few days. Yet she was angry to think that he should try such a cheap ploy to gain her gratitude. Surely she had made it clear that her gratitude would not extend so far? She plucked miserably at the fur trim on her jacket.

'Don't do that!' he said sharply, turning on her all of a sudden. 'You've no right to be wearing that jacket.'

Now it was her turn to question. 'What did you say?' she breathed.

Barron shrugged. '*Ayurnamat.*' He moved abruptly to the door.

Ayurnamat—it doesn't matter, it can't be helped. Belinda heard him leave with tears in her eyes. Suddenly, overwhelmingly, she had a desperate need to call him back, to feel his arms round her and again to feel the burning passion of his lips on hers. The futility of such wanting welled up inside her. It brought more tears. '*Ayurnamat,*' she whispered to herself. '*It can't be helped.*'

CHAPTER EIGHT

BELINDA washed herself and cleaned her teeth in water from a kettle of melted snow, then set about brushing her tangled mass of hair until it shone again. For the first time since leaving the settlement she felt well enough, and had the opportunity, to try and make something of her appearance. Barron had forbidden her to leave the snow house except for necessary calls of nature and she had spent an idle morning pottering about over the cooking, even ineffectually sweeping the floor with the back of Barron's huge snow knife, and trying to remember some of the cats' cradles Taqaq had taught her. Barron had come in when she was absorbed in a particularly intricate one and had abruptly told her to stop. She had looked up in amazement.

'Why on earth——' she began, a flush of irritation coming into her cheeks.

'Because,' he explained patiently, as if speaking to a child, 'it's not done to make them during daylight hours. It's something saved for the long dark nights in winter.'

That, and what else? she thought, biting the words back in the nick of time, as he had gently unwound the string from around her fingers. 'Anyway, that's wrong,' he told her. 'You should have looped it round the index fingers first.' Briefly their fingers had touched, and Belinda backed away at the contact as if scalded. She had let her breath come out sharply.

'Why is it you always think you're right about everything?' she demanded.

'Maybe because I nearly always am,' he replied without modesty. She was about to expostulate when she noticed the teasing gleam in his eye. It faded at once and the old coolness came between them again.

Because she was bored and fed-up with her vow of silence, she longed to have a good chat. Anything would be better than more unending hours of this icy silence. Barron seemed to be quite happy to go about his few chores without a word, and it piqued her to realise that her demonstration of indifference didn't seem to bother him in the least. Now that she was feeling more confident that he had no designs on her she quite irrationally wanted to arouse some response from him. He was busily scraping snow off his boots near the door when she spoke. 'You must know you make me feel like part of the furniture,' she said accusingly.

'I thought that was what you wanted?' he replied at once without bothering to look up. Belinda bit her lip.

'As it looks as if we're stuck with each other for a while you could try treating me like a human being,' she continued. He glanced across with a quizzical look in his eyes.

'That seemed to be the last thing you wanted from me,' he answered. 'I suppose you've changed your mind yet again.' For a moment they regarded each other belligerently across the freshly swept floor of snow.

Belinda felt a rush of colour when she met his eyes. This time she did not avert her own glance, but faced him steadily with clenched fists. 'It's your own fault. You always seem to provoke me. You make me so angry with the things you say. You must do it on purpose.'

'I can assure you I do no such things,' he replied cuttingly. 'I have no time for silly games like that.'

'You see! You're doing it again. Trying to make me look small.' She squared up to him with flushed cheeks.

'You are quite small,' he replied coolly. He took one of her hands in one of his. 'Quite small.' He let her hand drop. Belinda hesitated. Whatever she said next would have to be carefully chosen. They were suddenly on dangerous ground again. She took a breath. 'You say things, and I don't know what you mean by them.'

'Like what?' he demanded.

She turned away, picking at the sleeve of her parka. 'Well, about this jacket for one,' she raised her eyes accusingly. 'You said this thing about the jacket Mac gave me, and walked off without any explanation. Why haven't I got a right to wear it?' It hadn't been exactly what she wanted to say to him, but it was the safest thing she could think of, and she felt he owed her some explanation for his earlier remark. He seemed to stiffen and for a moment his eyes refused to meet hers.

'Please,' she said, 'why won't you explain?'

Carefully and with a degree of deliberation Barron fastened up his boots again, then moved casually over to where she was sitting on the platform and lowered himself down beside her. 'O.K. It doesn't really matter—I told you that. I was being weak. I was suffering from a pang of sentimentality, if you like.'

'You?' she broke in. The tautness in his face made the laughter fade as soon as it had pealed out. There was sheer pain in his face, in the twist of his lips, the rigidity of his jaw, in the brooding darkness of his eyes, as he flashed her a glance that made her shrivel inside.

'Yes, me,' he said harshly. 'Is that so strange?' The face he turned towards her had savagery written all over it. A primitive emotion seemed to etch deep lines on each side of his mouth. 'Life here has its pain, the pain of birth and death, like anywhere else,' he told her fiercely. 'I didn't come here to opt out of anything, if that's what you think. Relationships here are more intense, more real, than anything in your world. Someone who skims the surface like you, playing with men's emotions, won't understand what I mean. But here things have more meaning than in so-called civilised society where everything, even love, has a price tag on it.' For a moment he paused as if struggling in the grip of some fierce and painful emotion. He gave a

slow sideways glance at the jacket she was wearing and
his lips curled as he spoke: 'To you I suppose that's just a
nice, fur-lined jacket, not quite in the height of this year's
fashion. In reality it's something over which a man de-
monstrated the highest qualities of courage and endu-
rance, all the truest and most honourable virtues of friendship—no!——' his voice tailed off. When he spoke again
it was resonant with the force of his emotion. 'It was
something much more than friendship as you would
understand the word——' he broke off again, his words
fading into silence. His face was bleak in the desolation of
some unspoken memory.

Belinda sensed that the man he had obliquely referred
to was this sort of friend, and that something terrible had
happened. She watched his face with eyes that yearned to
share his grief, to ease the pain of his memory whatever it
was, but the delicacy of the moment was impossible to
translate into words. Vainly she sought for some means of
showing that she wanted to offer what comfort she could.
It made her put one hesitant hand on Barron's shoulder.
For a long moment his pained glance held hers, then the
familiar shuttered look came down, the cruel glint of some
sensation bordering on contempt sparked there and he
pushed her hand roughly aside. 'Stop your games,' he
sneered. 'I'm not putting on an act, I'm not begging for
sympathy. I don't get my women into bed that way.'

Belinda's cheeks flamed. 'I didn't mean——' She
stopped, a sort of despairing anger flooding through her
body so that her voice shook when she spoke. 'How can
you talk about real relationships, about friendships, when
you see everything in such horrid terms? What makes you
so sure that relationships here are so much deeper than in
my world? I feel pain too,' she glared.

He looked oddly at her, his lips twisting in a half-smile
that owed nothing to humour. 'Would you lay down your
life for me?' he asked simply. Before she could reply he
had thrown himself back full length on the bearskin and

closed his eyes. 'I'll tell you something about the inter-
relatedness of the people here,' he said. 'If you change
your mind about accepting my offer of help when you
meet the Nasaq, you'll have to know something about
friendship patterns in order to make sense of their social
structure.'

'You're talking like a sociologist,' she said absent-
mindedly, still occupied with the answer to his last
question.

'Heaven forbid!' He gave a short laugh and his eyes
narrowed. She was very conscious of the long length of his
form as he reclined easily beside her on the platform. His
deerskins failed to conceal the huskiness of his frame, the
sense of vibrant health which his hard outdoor life had
given him, and it brought a tremor to her so that she felt
a pang when she realised that her answer to his question
might just be yes. He would be a man worth making any
sacrifice for—she shuddered. That was a dangerous
thought in present circumstances. If Barron guessed she
was into the self-sacrifice business ten to one it wouldn't
be death he would demand of her. His blue eyes were just
chips of ice between the narrow slits of his eyelids. She felt
his glance sweep over her and a shiver ran uncontrollably
over her body.

'Cold?' he asked, without moving.

'No—it's nothing. Just a ghost, maybe,' she laughed
shakily to cover her confusion.

'Maybe I should have given you the full treatment after
such a severe chill,' he said with an amused smile.

'What's that?' she asked.

'Stripping and a good rub down all over,' he replied.
'Perhaps that's what you need now?'

'No!' she said violently, muscles tensing. 'I'm all right.
I don't feel cold any more.'

He laughed softly. 'Only in your heart, perhaps,
nothing will melt that. The job comes first.'

She raised eyes to him which were large with unshed

tears. 'I wish you'd stop saying things like that to me. Just because I'm not willing to become an exchange partner——' she faltered.

'Oh, so you know about those?' he broke in mockingly. 'You must have been doing some homework, like a good little girl. Derek will be pleased with you.'

'Derek?' she queried in bewilderment.

'Isn't that the man who sent you out here? Isn't he the reason you've been so tenacious in your attempts to meet the Nasaq? You don't want to let Derek down.' He smiled grimly. 'He must mean quite a lot to you.'

'No, that's not it at all,' she said. 'It's not like that—at least, not now.' She flushed hotly and her words petered out. She knew quite well what the real reason was for Derek offering her the assignment in preference to anyone else in the department. Of course she was as capable as any one of them, and certainly as well qualified, but she was fully aware that it was Derek's personal feelings for her which had tipped the scales in her favour. If he had not felt that the relationship was becoming a threat to the stability of his marriage, to his career even, he would have never let her go.

'Or perhaps he'd finished with you and you're trying to get back into his favour,' said Barron cruelly.

'You would paint a black picture, wouldn't you?' she retorted. 'You always try to make me look worse than I really am. It wasn't like that at all. Derek hasn't finished with me. He gave me this opportunity because—because——'

'So he hasn't finished with you? I don't for one minute believe any man could finish with you once he'd loved you,' he said, quietly.

Nonplussed, Belinda pushed a lock of hair out of her eyes. 'Can't we keep this on a practical level?' she asked curtly. 'I thought you were going to tell me something about kinship patterns or something?'

Barron let his eyelids close. In a flat, unemotional voice

he began to detail the different bonds which existed between members of the same group. 'Exchange partners
you seem to know about. Seal partners—does that mean
anything to you?' Belinda remembered the first time, it
seemed ages ago now, when Mac had used the phrase.
She had intended to ask him then what it meant but had
forgotten about it in the rush of new sensations she had
experienced in her first days in the Arctic. Now she shook
her head.

'When the white fox trapping season ends in March,'
Barron told her, 'all the Eskimos who've been living out
on the traplines drift back to the post to turn in their pelts
and trade for the things they need for the coming season.'

'Is that why you're here now?' she asked, 'living near
your traplines?'

He nodded. 'I'm not staying out here until March,
though. I'll drift back in a while, as Ikluk is pregnant.'

An icy hand clutched Belinda's heart and for a moment
it was as if her breath was stopped. She looked urgently
at Barron.

He seemed unaware of the bombshell he had dropped,
and was lying back among the bearskins, eyes closed,
tanned face conveying no recognition of the painful blow
he had so casually inflicted.

Pregnant? That must explain the way one of the women
had made Ikluk replace the large box she had been
atempting to carry up to the store shed on ship-day. That
would explain too the familiar ring to her voice when she
had called out to Barron that day when she had passed
Belinda in the copse. No wonder she had sounded at
home! She had been like any woman anywhere, returning
to her husband after a morning's shopping, only in this
case she had been at an Eskimo trading post and the
shopping seemed to be caribou skins.

Belinda shut her eyes against the sudden access of pain
that shot through her body. It was with an ache that she
realised that despite her repugnance at Barron's apparent

casual promiscuity and the knowledge that he was unfree to form any attachment except on a casual exchange basis, she wanted him with a fierce and overpowering hunger which was entirely new to her.

He had opened his eyes and was again looking oddly into her face. 'Are you sure you're feeling all right?' he asked carelessly.

'Stop fussing!' she burst out angrily. 'Of course I'm all right. What on earth do you mean?'

Barron shrugged. 'Have you been listening to what I've been saying?' he demanded.

'Some of it,' she admitted truthfully.

'What did I say a break in the sea ice was called?'

She shrugged irritably. 'How on earth can I be expected to remember every fiddling little word in this lousy language?' she burst out, glowering at him, heart twisting with pain as he grinned lazily back at her.

'You're the person who once said it was precious and beautiful and unique,' he told her, the amusement making his eyes sparkle wickedly.

'Did I say that?' She hated him. 'That was then, wasn't it?' she retorted. 'I felt different then.'

'Did you?' he breathed. 'Belinda——' he sat up suddenly and caught hold of her by the wrist. She trembled at his touch and tried to pull away. 'I'm not going to hurt you.' He pushed her hair back from her face. 'Has something made you change?' he asked. 'Don't you think it's precious and beautiful and unique any more?'

Her thoughts were running in all directions in the confusion of his nearness. She tried vainly to steady herself by fixing her gaze on a point just past his left ear lobe.

'Look at me,' he insisted gently, turning her face up to his. 'You must know that I've changed. Something's happened to me. Now it's you that seems to be all those things.' Slowly he bent to kiss her lips.

Belinda felt the resistance drain away in the ecstasy of

his touch. There was no rhyme or reason in it. The very hair of his head seemed to carry an electric charge as it brushed her face and she wanted to cry out in the sweet anguish of her longing. With an effort of will she made herself push him away, allowing her mind to dwell on the inevitable bitterness and regret in the future if she succumbed now to the urgent desire of the moment.

She turned blazing eyes on him.

'Now? Yes! You can say that now! While you've got me a prisoner out here, miles from anywhere. You can say that to me now, can't you? Where no one can see, where no one knows what you're saying!'

Barron let his hands drop from her as if stung. 'Am I too clumsy or what? I hoped you were beginning to feel——'

'Feel what? Randy?' she asked through tight lips. 'You really thought I was going to say yes? You thought all it needed was a few pretty words, a little flattery, and I'd be stupid enough to fall for it?' She laughed with derision to hide the hollowness in her heart. 'You're contemptible!' The expression on his face wrung her heart. It made her swing back on him even more fiercely. 'Don't look at me like that—I can't stand it. It's a game with you. You want to have me as casually as your other partners.' The thought of Ikluk filled her eyes with scalding tears, but she turned away blindly, scrubbing her knuckles into them so that he would not see. 'I want you to leave me alone,' she said in a fierce quiet voice. 'I told you at the beginning that I have no interest in you. I find your way of life and sense of values beneath contempt.' She heard him give a slight movement behind her and next moment she turned to see him sinking back among the furs. He didn't look at her.

'Seal partners, then.' He spoke in a schoolmasterly way, rapidly and dryly, explaining how in the summer months a group of five or six men, armed only with harpoons, would take their loaded freight sled up to the ice floes of the northern seas, there to hunt the seal. She felt like saying that she didn't want to hear about it, that she thought it cruel and barbaric, but when Barron explained that the ancient method was part of the Eskimo's fight for survival, that it was no different, in fact probably more humane, than civilised man's way of dealing with beef or mutton or any other staple of his diet, she began to understand more of what he was trying to say.

His anger against the white man who regularly culled seals barbarously with clubs and guns was plain to see, and again she saw the cold come into his eyes which made them resemble chipped ice. He does have standards, she thought miserably, even if he's perfectly willing to be unfaithful to his pregnant wife and to take his sexual gratification when and where he can.

His voice seemed like music to her ears even though he was telling her in clinical detail every incident in a typical hunt. He spared her nothing, telling how they would poke down through the ice with a special snow probe, how, when they had found a suitable seal hole, they would set up the harpoon in line with the place where the seal would appear, how the lures were set, how they themselves would then settle down on the ice to wait, perhaps for hours, perhaps for a whole day.

He told how the sun would burn the face, and how it was necessary to keep still so as not to scare the seal by making shadows on the ice. Belinda asked him what he thought about all day in that long unbroken solitude of waiting.

'It's a good time, then,' he told her, a faraway look coming into his eyes. 'It's the time for making up songs to sing later at the drum dance.'

'Your world—it's so different from mine, isn't it?'

'If you behave yourself I'll take you to a drum dance.' His words were light, but he watched her warily. 'May I take you dancing, ma'am?'

She couldn't fathom his thoughts when his eyes had

that lazy, dangerous glint to them.

'The Nasaq will be arriving soon. It will be bad manners not to accept their invitation to the dance.'

'I wouldn't dream of refusing,' she told him, shrugging unconcernedly. She would do as he said so far as the Nasaq were concerned. That was work. She told him so, and he smiled again with a strange look.

'I've already gathered that you'll do almost anything in the name of research,' he said. He spoke in such a way that she coloured hotly. As if not wishing to tread dangerous ground, Barron resumed his schoolmasterish tone and began to recount the ritual which took place whenever a first seal was caught. He told her how it was bad manners for the hunter to look too happy when the other men clustered round to congratulate him, and how he had had to explain to the others how hopeless he was, that it was purely luck that he had caught a seal, that if he had been a better hunter he would have got a much bigger seal. Belinda's eyes opened wider.

'Do you mean you've actually done all this?'

His lean face had been averted from hers throughout this story, but now he turned it briefly towards her. Once again his look was difficult to fathom. 'Did you think I'd got it all out of books?' he asked sardonically.

'Well, I find it difficult to imagine you looking humble,' she replied tartly.

His eyes crinkled in a brief grin. 'It was difficult. I was feeling pretty pleased with myself that first time. It was like having one's first woman,' he added brutally, watching her expression. 'We were all shouting and laughing as we put the seal on to the sled and dragged it back to camp.' He paused.

'What happened next? Did you cook it and eat it then and there?'

'No. There's another part of the ritual.' He had a thoughtful look in his eyes. 'One of the women had to pour fresh water into its mouth and singe the whiskers

with a piece of birch bark. Again it's part of the ancient
ritual——'

'Women?' Belinda interrupted. 'I didn't realise women
went hunting too.'

'They come out with us, but don't involve themselves
with the actual hunt. It's useful,' he went on, still watching her closely, 'to have a woman back in the snow house
after a day on the ice.'

I bet it is, thought Belinda grimly, biting off the cutting
response that sprang immediately to her lips. She gazed
moodily at the toes of her own sealskin boots.

Barron went on talking, unperturbed. 'After she's per-
formed various ceremonies it's time to get your partners.'

Belinda wished she could shut her ears to what he was
saying. She didn't want a blow-by-blow account of his sex
life.

He eyed her speculatively before he went on. 'When a
man kills a seal, he has to divide it up with his partners.
According to custom there are about sixteen or seventeen
portions to a carcase and they have to be given to each of
the hunter's partners.'

'You mean you have sixteen or seventeen partners?'
burst out Belinda incredulously. She eyed him with
blank-eyed astonishment. No wonder he preferred this
primitive life in the Arctic wilds if such customs were the
norm!

He laughed softly. 'Up in arms again?' he derided. 'You
sound as if it matters to you.'

'I couldn't care less how many partners you have, as
long as none of them are me,' she told him frigidly. 'Have
twenty, have a hundred. It's nothing to me. I'm just surprised that you actually have time to do any hunting!'

He threw his head back at this. 'Oh, Belinda, you are
sweet.' His eyes teased hers, but she refused to be melted.
'These partners are seal partners. They're the men who've
taken part in the hunt,' he explained. 'One of them will
be a heart partner, one a rib partner and so on. The idea

is that whenever a seal is killed every man in the group will get a portion. No one will go without. It's a way of making sure no one goes hungry.' He smiled. 'You still have a long way to go before you revise your opinions about these people,' he told her, 'and,' he added, 'about me too.'

Belinda flushed. 'You deliberately led me to believe—oh, what's the point?' she finished abruptly. 'You've never denied that you have that sort of relationship.'

'What sort?' he persisted, widening his eyes innocently. She threw him a furious glance which was answer enough.

'I'm a man. And if I have that sort of relationship, is it any business of yours?' He watched closely for her response.

'Certainly not!' was the immediate reply. 'It has no interest for me whatsoever.'

Barron sighed and looked thoughtful for a moment.

'You're so censorious, Belinda.' He looked as if he was going to go on and say something else and a frown knit his brow, but instead he eased himself into another position and locked his hands behind his head. 'Another thing about seal partnerships is that they're hereditary,' he went on after a short pause. 'It seems to be the only relationship that is. That means that if I have a son, he will inherit all the partnerships I've had,' he told her. 'He will be heart partner to the son of my heart partner.'

Belinda let the words re-echo in her mind. 'He will be——' Barron had said. 'Will be.' It was already a foregone conclusion, then. He had really and truly turned native. Not only did he have exchange partners and hunting relationships, he was already thinking into the future when his own children would inherit the same hard and primitive way of life that he had so unaccountably picked out for himself.

'Why *did* you choose to live here of all places?' she asked involuntarily. As soon as she had uttered the words she could have bitten off her tongue. She didn't want to know anything else about him, anything that would make her think any the less of him. His chosen way of life was so difficult to understand, she felt frightened at the thought of hearing any more.

Instead of replying all at once, Barron lay still for a moment with his head thrown back and his eyes shut. The sharply etched outlines of his deeply tanned face looked stern. With a glance full of longing flooding her expression now that he was no longer watching her, Belinda traced from a distance with her eyes the shape of his cheekbones over which the skin, taut and weathered by the fierce northern winds, glowed with health, and virility in the soft light of the soapstone lamp. His dark brows arched aristocratically over deep-set eyes, the arrogantly straight nose seemed to foretell the hint of savagery in the set of the mouth, yet in all this strength and unyieldingness, in all this obvious power and will to dominate, there was a fine sensitivity, a hint of gentleness which seemed wildly at variance with what she already knew of his present way of life and what she suspected of his past. There was even, she thought, a hint of vulnerability about him, a hint of the poet and dreamer. When his face was in repose as now, surely, she argued hopelessly with herself, it must have been the poet, the idealist in the man which had made him reject ordinary society? Surely it wasn't anything dishonourable that had brought him here? She waited for what he would confess, fearful that her fantasy was about to be destroyed by a confession of villainy which would once again put her in fear for herself, alone and defenceless, as she was in this desolate place.

Suddenly his eyes snapped open, taking her unawares with their startling clarity of blue. His tone was expressionless and he smiled lazily but without humour. 'Why am I here? Wouldn't you like to know?' His lips curled bitterly. 'I thought you knew I was a renegade, on the run from the past.' His eyes swept her body in that openly

appraising way which had made her blood boil on their
very first meeting.

'It's all right,' she said quickly, fearing to arouse any
uncontrollable passions connected directly with his secret
past. '*Ayurnamat.*'

Barron smiled at her use of the Eskimo word. 'We'll
make a native of you yet!' His eyes closed once more, and
he seemed to drift off into thoughts and memories of the
past which brought him no pleasure, for his jaw was set
rigidly and his lips formed a tight line of determination as
if he had become used to the need to battle in both his
previous life in the world of big cities and business, as well
as here in nature's cruel world of ice and snow and unending darkness.

Belinda longed with all her heart to be able to see into
his soul, to fathom the heart of this man whose abrupt
silences and self-mocking seemed to hint at a deep and
hidden sorrow.

He spoke no more that evening. It was as if he had
clammed up on some brooding secret in his inner self.
Belinda sensed that he needed to remain within himself,
that talk was anathema to him in his present mood and
she respected the silence he seemed to draw around himself like a cone. Wordlessly she had lain under the caribou
blanket, and when Barron had risen from his place on the
platform to put out the lamp she had stared into the
darkness at the place where she could hear him tossing
and turning in a fretful sleep. It was several long hours
before sleep at last overtook her too.

Next day it was so dark when Belinda woke up that
only the sense that a certain number of hours had elapsed
since she had fallen into a belated insensibility told her
that a new day had arrived. Barron had already risen, as
if in possession of some kind of highly-developed, animal
sense of the passage of time and the changing of night
into day. She knew he never wore a watch.

Now she could see the glow from the approaching lamp

and tensed at the soft scraping sounds of his boots on the snow as he came quietly into the snow house. He moved as if he didn't want to wake her and for a time he simply held the lamp up high, checking, it seemed to her, that everything was in order. Then he busied himself with the heater and the cooking pot.

'They're arriving already,' he said without turning round. Belinda sat up on one arm.

'How did you know I was awake?' she asked.

'Have you slept much?' He turned his glance full on her as if searching for the answer to some other question.

She shook her head. 'I don't know why not. I couldn't settle,' she replied.

'Nor could I,' he replied.

She swung her legs energetically over the edge of the platform. 'Am I going to be allowed out today?' she demanded.

'I should hope so,' he smiled. 'You've had a long enough holiday. Now it's time to start work. Got your tape-recorder?'

An unexpected feeling of anticipation took hold of her. 'Do you really mean that?' she said, scarcely believing what he was implying. 'And why have you changed your mind? You've been obstructing me for so long, what's made you change?'

'Stop asking irrelevant questions. Eat your breakfast, then come on out,' he ordered. 'I'll show you to them, then you can decide how you want to work. It might be a good idea to ask someone to describe the building of a snow house as they do it, as their methods are quite unique, and then you can tape the whole process of setting up camp, from the beginning, then tape something on the different daily chores, and so on. Unless——' he looked down at the tousle-headed girl with a mocking glance, 'unless you stick by what you said earlier. About not wanting my help?'

Belinda had the grace to look ashamed. 'Words spoken

in anger,' she told him with a rueful smile. 'I do forgive
and forget sometimes.'

'So do I!' he said with a note of grimness in his voice.
'Life would be impossible otherwise.' Briefly a shadow
seemed to cross his face. 'Come on,' he chided her, as if
making an effort to escape the mood of the previous night.
'The time is now and now is the time! Buck up!'

Belinda got quickly to her feet. She was in no mood to
point out how bossy he was this morning. There was too
much to do.

She exchanged a smile with him as she washed and
dried herself in a hurried attempt to freshen up. It certainly wouldn't have done if she'd been over-fussy about
her appearance. A quick brushing of her hair tamed the
shining mass of gold into some semblance of style and in a
moment she came to stand to attention in front of him.
'All present and correct, sir!' she joked.

For a moment he seemed arrested by something about
her. A word of approval escaped him, then he turned his
head abruptly. 'Too beautiful,' he said. His mouth curved
in a crooked grin when he looked back at her. 'What am I
to tell them when they ask me if I want to share you?'

Belinda coloured violently. 'Surely they won't think
that we——' she halted in confusion.

'Will it bother you?' he asked, paused on the threshold,
ready to go out.

'They must know about——' Colour flooded her cheeks
again. 'I mean, what will they think of me——?' It wasn't
what she had meant to say. She glanced quickly at him to
see if he was teasing, but his face was serious.

'It's bad manners for a man to refuse any request from
his seal partners,' he told her seriously. Belinda picked up
her recording equipment and made for the door.

'You know what I think,' she told him through tight
lips. The last thing she wanted was to get into another
argument with him at this stage. They would just have to
agree to differ and he would have to tell his precious

partners she was not for barter.

Later that day Belinda was feeling happier about her work than she would have ever thought possible over the last few weeks. Barron was an excellent guide and translator, seeming to possess the ability to predict her needs at any time. He was also discreet and kept himself well in the background so that her subjects were free to give her all the information she might require.

After a long session with the group of men building a house he told her that it was time for a rest, but that as they were going to eat in the house of the shaman she should bring the tape-recorder and see if he would give permission for her to record some of his songs. 'If not,' he told her, 'you can record the communal songs in the snow house during the drum dance tonight. I told you I'd take you dancing. I hope you're not going to turn me down?'

She shrugged and avoided his glance. 'Where on earth can they have a dance?' she asked instead. There was a note of mystification in her voice, for none of the family houses were big enough to cope with more than three or four visitors, and the whole community here was close to fifty adults plus a tangle of excited children who seemed to be everywhere at once.

'Wait and see,' was his only reply as he ushered her forward to meet the shaman.

Belinda briefly wondered how he had described her when he made the introductions. The shaman's dark eyes had glittered in a friendly fashion as he turned to her, saying her name over to himself, as if testing the syllables in his mouth and letting his sharp-eyed glance take in everything about her. Now, while they talked, she had a chance to let her gaze rest lingeringly on Barron's strong intelligent face, and she noted with tenderness that it was suffused with such an expression of warmth and interest as he spoke to his friends that he seemed to be a totally different man from the sombre, taciturn one who had shut her out of his memories so emphatically the previous night. He seemed to be truly at one with those nomads, loved and accepted into their close-knit community with no reservations. Belinda had been moved by a feeling which she was beginning to recognise as something like respect for this man when she saw how he had been greeted by every single adult in the party as they had driven up on their sleds, and even round-faced children had flocked around him, as if he was a favourite uncle, following in his wake, imitating his every move, the smallest ones clambering all over him whenever the chance arose. His appearance seemed to cause a stir like that of a returning hero—so much so, that she had turned impulsively to him at one point and asked him if they were always so friendly and exuberant in their dealings with outsiders.

'I'm not an outsider,' he said simply. 'And because you're with me, neither are you. They all like you very much.'

Belinda looked abashed. 'They seemed to have such a reputation for shyness, coldness even,' she replied. 'I'm just surprised that they seem so wonderfully open-hearted.'

He had smiled wryly, his voice grim. 'Not many people take the trouble to get to know them as well as I have. They've had some nasty experiences with white folk. They're wise to be on their guard. I've been very lucky, very privileged, in my dealings with them.'

She had wanted to question him further, maybe even ask about the man whom he had thought of as a friend, but it seemed wiser to let no dark shadows from the past spoil the present mood of gaiety which was growing with every new arrival to the map.

'Isn't this better than your artificial city life?' Barron had murmured, brushing her hair once, as if by accident, with his lips.

She had declined to answer, but found it difficult to move away. She had let his lips press her forehead before moving slowly out of reach.

Certainly she could see now why he had tried to protect these people from what he thought was a crude incursion from the outside world by a scandal-hungry sociologist.

Now the shaman was saying something to her, and Barron leaned across and touched her arm. 'He wants you to show him how the tape recorder works.'

By the time Belinda had been entertained by the couple, and had spent a couple of hours recording and playing back their voices on the recorder to enormous roars of laughter, it was late in the afternoon. From the air of excitement which seemed to pervade the camp she guessed something special was about to happen. Barron led her outside to look, and she was amazed to see the finishing touches being put to a large snow house, so high that the men were standing on oil drums in order to put the finishing blocks in the roof.

'Our palais de danse,' said Barron with a grin. 'Don't forget we have a date tonight.'

Without thinking Belinda slipped her arm in his. 'But I've got nothing to wear,' she teased.

He gave her a strange look. 'I think it'll be come-as-you-are,' he told her, taking her hand tightly in his for a moment.

Night came at last. The children were put quickly to bed, and it was time for the drum dance. Everyone by now was in a good mood as they crowded together in the snow house. Barron explained as best he could in the babble of voices that the point of the drum dance lay not in the beating of the drum but in the words of the songs.

'When somebody sings they sing their own personal song, and it's always the story of some true happening in their life, something important from their own experience. A man's wife may sing his song, but no one else can unless he gives them permission, though two men may become song partners and exchange songs so that they sing about each other's exploits. That way they can overcome their modesty about their own exploits.'

'Do you have a song partner as well?' asked Belinda curiously. But before he could answer a man suddenly leapt into an empty space in the middle of the crowd and started to beat a drum like a huge tambourine, swinging it from side to side, beating out the rhythm, jumping and turning in the beginnings of a primitive dance.

Soon everyone was joining in, shouting encouragement, leaping to their feet to keep time with the heady insistence of the rhythm being pounded out without a break. When one man tired another would snatch up the tambourine and continue with his own song or that of his partner, so that the crowd was kept continually dancing and clapping out the beat. The drummer started to sing the words of his song in a weird, piercing, primitive voice, choosing a woman he had had his eye on to direct it to.

Belinda struggled to set up her tape recorder, but the dance was really getting going now, the temperature was rising and people, already having stripped off their heavy deerskin outer garments, were beginning to strip to their waists.

At first Belinda averted her eyes when she saw the first woman taking off her soft leather tunic, but in the excited crush of bodies she soon found that all her attention was needed to hang on to the tape recorder. It seemed pointless to bother about sound levels and she simply pointed the microphone into the middle of the throng. Barron eyed her struggles with one eyebrow raised sardonically, but had offered no help until a man, snatching the drum from one of his wildly spinning companions, began to dance provocatively in front of Belinda, directing the words of his song at her. She raised helpless eyes to Barron, but he had his handsome face thrown back in a broad smile. His only response had been to press the off-switch of the recorder, pushing her forward into the crowd with the words: 'Go on, let your hair down for once. Get up and dance with him.'

Everyone was so excited and caught up in the music that she was soon dancing as uninhibitedly as the rest of them. It was as if some spirit of the dance had caught hold of her and she had become enslaved by it. Vaguely she remembered seeing Barron take the drum and his strong, masculine voice had rung out with the strangely primitive sounds of his paean. Briefly she wondered what event they commemorated, but she soon lost him in the crowd as her partner led her into the fray.

It seemed as if they danced for hours, locked in the intensity of the primitive drumbeats. Belinda's hair was sticking to the nape of her neck and she knew her cheeks were flushed with a new and bewitching excitement. She thought Barron was lost for good when her partner started to lead her off through the crush to the side where piles of discarded garments were strewn near the door, but at once Barron was beside her, singing his words, now plaintively and caressingly, now shouting them out in triumph as he reached the climax, exulting in the event they recorded, in the secret which lay in the primitive sound.

Almost before he had finished he had thrust the drum into the hands of Belinda's partner so that the man became the focus for the excitement of the dancers. With the beat of the drum throbbing out in such frenzy it seemed that the words themselves didn't matter much any more.

Barron swung Belinda back into the thick of the crowd, his arms strong about her waist, his face pressing up against her hair. She had time to notice that one or two couples were discreetly leaving the dancing and making their way outside, but only when Barron, his body taut against her own, started to propel her too in the direction of the door did she look up at him in alarm.

Instead of letting her speak he pressed his lips roughly against her own and with the heat of the dancers and the excitement of the throbbing drumbeat she felt her resistance to him seeping away. He half carried, half walked

her towards the door, but she wasn't so deeply bewitched
by the music of the last few hours that she didn't notice
that people moved aside deferentially for him and that
the smiles which passed from face to face were indulgent,
even if knowing.

'Please, Barron, no!' she whispered weakly as she felt
his hard body pressing against her own. His lips once
again searched hungrily for hers as they had done that
time near the store shed in the settlement. This time,
though, no memories can to rescue her from the sea of
emotion which was flooding over her and it was with a
sense of dazed shock that she found herself wrapped in his
arms, and being led, stumbling across the snow, towards
their own snow house. It was now surrounded by other
houses from some of which subdued laughter and the
murmuring of the newcomers were clearly audible. Once
inside Belinda felt herself being pushed gently down on to
the silky furs heaped on the sleeping platform and in a
daze she could feel their sensuous luxury against her
skin. Although it was pitch dark she could sense that
Barron had taken off some of his own clothing, and her
hands sought for contact with the smooth muscularity of
his body. His own hands imperiously explored her as she
began to moan in ecstasy beneath his touch. It was as she
clung to him, begging him to take her, to do what he
wanted with her, that all the pent-up misery of loving a
man who could never be hers began to well up inside her,
and the hot tears of her despair began to course uncontrollably down her cheeks. Desperately she clung to
him, locks of blonde hair wetly sticking to her tear-stained
face as she struggled beneath the kisses he showered on
her face and neck. Gently he cupped her breasts in his
hands, bringing his head down again and again to mas-
sage the soft flesh with his lips. The tears were coursing
now without cease down her face and little by little she
started to try to free herself from his urgent embrace. She
felt herself torn in an agony of wanting and fearing that

left her struggling breathlessly against the yearning of his body. When he started to unfasten her boots so that he could slip her pants off she managed to pull herself up into a sitting position and tried in vain to push his hands away, but his mouth came down again, seeking some answering passion, and again and again she tried to beat ineffectually against his broad back, but her fists seemed like toys against the contained power of his muscles.

In a frenzy now of despair and confusion, yearning for him, yet in anguish at the knowledge that she was a mere plaything to him, she began to bite and scratch, twisting and turning in her efforts to escape. Barron seemed to think it was some sort of game, for his kisses became even more passionate and it was only when she called out that he recognised the genuine anguish in her voice.

For a moment he fell back as if stunned, but it was enough. With one bound she was across to the door and, snatching up her parka, she was running outside into the cold night air before he could even bring her name to his lips.

She was already half-way across the encampment before he managed to get outside, and then it was a mad race across the snow.

She had no idea where she was running to, she simply knew that she had to get away, she had to flee, she had to escape the dreadful pain that the night would bring if she remained with him. Feverishly she darted behind a snow house, but he saw her and came running after her, calling her name in bewilderment and with a rising note of anger in it.

She forced herself on, twisting among the houses until she came to the edge of the camp, then there was just the open desolation of the snowy landscape ahead. It seemed to echo the desolation in her heart and mind. She ran on into it, gulping in great sobbing breaths of the thin Arctic air.

Soon the sound of her breathing and the steady crunch of her boots on the ice were the only sounds she could hear.

CHAPTER NINE

'My darling, please speak to me . . .' The anguish and concern in his face was not something that could be imitated without the presence of genuine emotion. Belinda looked at him in wonder, her face tracing the lines at the corners of his mouth, her fingers touching briefly the lock of dark hair which fell over his forehead. Without anger she idly wondered how he could look at her with eyes so filled with love when his own wife was about to bear him a child. She contemplated his face with the detachment which comes from taking a heavy sleeping draught and, bewildered, she let her glance slide past him to the neat, bright room, with its hospital trolley, its vases of flowers, and its clinical apparatus gleamingly arrayed against the plainly painted wall. She felt so tired, so unreal, but when her glance came back to rest on the face of the man sitting so anxiously by her side, she let one word like a small sigh of contentment escape her lips.

'*Amaruq*,' she breathed. The name brought a sleepy smile to her face.

It was several hours later when the effects of the drug had worn off that she was at last fully awake to hear the story of her rescue by a search party made up from revellers at the drum dance.

Amaruq, for that was how she now somehow thought of him, had lost sight of her among the maze of snow houses, and by the time he had had time to fasten the laces of his boots in order to give chase, she had managed to escape from the camp altogether. A sudden blizzard,

though short-lived, had obliterated all trace of her footprints and men from the camp had been out all night
searching for her. It had been the sheer desperate persist-
ance of Amaruq himself in urging the men on that had led
them at last to the pathetic form lying huddled in the snow.

Amaruq didn't tell her how he had thrown himself
down beside her in a frenzy of despair, convinced that she
was dead, frozen to death in that cruel latitude, and how
he had flung off his own coat in an effort to warm her and
how the other men, forcing him back into it, had carried
Belinda between them, wrapped in caribou skins brought
from the camp.

'It was touch and go whether you would pull through,'
he told her sternly. 'That must surely go down in history
as the most stupid thing anybody has ever done.'

No, she thought to herself, suitably chastened by his
words, but following a train of thought of her own, the
most stupid thing was to fall for a man like you. But she
raised contrite eyes to him and let them dwell lovingly on
his face.

He was dressed in a black sweater and a plain duffle
jacket, his hair, shorter, brushed till it gleamed, and when
he came close there was the subtle tang of some after-
shave lotion. But his face was pale and drawn.

'What made you do it, darling? I don't understand.'
He took her hand gently. 'You seemed to want me so
much.' He paused. 'You must have known I wouldn't
have taken you against your will. The drum dance had
such a powerful effect I was finding it difficult to stop
myself. If you hadn't seemed so willing I wouldn't have
laid a finger on you.' He paused again and looked search-
ingly into her face. 'Tell me you wanted it too.'

For a moment Belinda couldn't reply. Her emotions
were too mixed up to allow for words. When she finally
raised her eyes to his, the answer was plain to read.

'Then why run away in such a panic? As if you were
frightened to death of me?'

She took a deep breath.

'Any girl would be frightened of a man called wolf,' she replied, averting her glance, hoping her voice would not falter in its attempted joke.

'There's something else,' said Barron, his face hardening. He made as if to get up.

'You've never bothered to tell me why—why that name,' she demanded.

He looked bored. 'The Eskimos are great ones for names. They believe they have magical properties. When a child is born a string of names are reeled out until it stops crying, then that name becomes its own for life. The only time a name is changed is if there's a brush with death. Then a new name has to be chosen.'

'Yes, but it's you I want to learn about,' she persisted, looking reproachfully at him. 'You never tell me anything about yourself. You always fob me off with sociology. Why, Amaruq? Did you have a brush with death? Is that why you've changed your name?'

He laughed shortly. 'Are you trying to be perceptive, Belinda?'

She looked steadily back at him from the pillow, her eyes brooking no escape this time. He put his hands in his pockets and half turned away to gaze out of the window. 'It's nothing really. I just happened to lay out a bully for the Nasaq. He'd been terrorising them for a long time. He pushed me a bit too far, that's all. I just taught him a lesson. From then on they called me Amaruq.' He grinned, turning back to the bed. 'Satisfied?'

'No,' she regarded him levelly. 'Why are you living this sort of life?'

His face took on a stubborn look. 'I wanted to be left alone. I'd had enough.' He wouldn't look at her. She waited to see if he would elaborate, but he turned away and seemed to become interested in a picture of mountain peaks and waterfalls hanging above the bed. 'But why do you want to be left alone?' she persisted softly.

He looked at her sardonically, one eyebrow raised. 'Did,' he said. 'Did . . . past tense.' A shadow passed momentarily across his face. 'Look, I've got to go. I'm getting a plane out to the post this morning, then I shall be travelling by sled to my traplines—they've been neglected too long. The nursing staff tell me you're going to be on your feet in a few days.' He looked critically at her. 'You'll have to behave yourself and do as they say. I don't know what your plans are. All your recording equipment is back at the trading post with Mac. If you need any help of any kind, get in touch with the shaman Nuallataq. He knows a little of the Nasaq speech patterns.' He paused and seemed to push his hands deeper into his jacket pockets. 'I guess this is it.'

The breath suddenly stopped in Belinda's throat. Before she could say anything he had moved swiftly over to the bed, kissed her lightly on the forehead and had headed swiftly out of the door. It closed behind him with a definitive click.

'Wait!' she called out, sitting up abruptly as if jerked into sudden life, but already the echo of his footsteps was fading down the corridor. In the silence left by his departure a million thoughts and emotions came crowding in upon her, but underneath it all an overpowering desolation seemed to take hold of her heart, and she knew, with a shudder of certainty, that there would be no forgetting.

Within a few days she was given a clean bill of health, and it wasn't long before she was stepping on to the tarmac at Inuvik airport to board the air charter company's snowplane back to Two Rivers. Chuck had been at her bedside constantly over the last couple of days, and when she chidingly said she thought he was supposed to be taking some leave about now, he teasingly told her that it had always been his ambition to holiday in a hospital – as a visitor, he hastened to add. They had one or two laughs while she was there and he had helped to speed her on

the road to recovery and take her mind off some of the
heartache she was suffering at the suddenness and finality
of Amaruq's goodbye. But it had not escaped the pilot
that Belinda had been unusually remote, not her old self
at all, and he had pondered over this in the privacy of his
thoughts throughout several long nights of broken sleep.

Meeting the trapper, Barron, charging down the hospital steps one morning had not helped to put Chuck's
mind at ease, and he had continued to brood on the
change in Belinda. In the little airport waiting-room just
now he had tactlessly seized the opportunity he had been
waiting for while they were briefly alone together to ask
her what was wrong. She had pleaded tiredness, but the
wan look she had given him had increased his suspicions.
He had taken her almost roughly by the shoulders as she
had stepped on ahead, and swinging her round to face
him he had put the question again.

'Something happened out there with Barron, didn't it?'
he demanded. Belinda had looked at him with startled
eyes, but the same remote expression as before had quickly
followed, and a sad smile briefly played across her face.

'I'm sorry, Chuck, I'm sorry.' Without explanation she
had disengaged herself from his grasp.

'If it was anything to do with that man . . .' He paused,
jealousy twisting his face into a momentarily unpleasant
mask.

'It's to do with me, and me alone,' she told him gently.
'Don't blame anyone else.' She turned wearily to pick up
her things. 'Are we going?'

Together they had flown in silence over the now glistening white terrain which lay between Invik and the
trading post. Its beauty would not so very long ago have
moved Belinda to cries of delight, but now she looked
dully at the frozen beauty of the landscape, with a similar
ice around her heart. Along with her love for Amaruq
had grown a quite firm and surprising love for the harsh
contours of this landscape, and although she told herself

that it was an unforgiving country, the kind of place that seldom gives man or woman a second chance, she knew it would be a special kind of heartbreak to leave it.

When the plane landed at Two Rivers there was quite a reception committee. Apart from the permanent staff on the settlement there were still several families who had stayed on to see Belinda again. The awkwardness between her and Chuck at first passed unnoticed, and it was only when he had told the Macs that he had to be getting back that Mrs Mac's face had grown suddenly perturbed. 'Why, Chuck,' she protested, 'I'd hoped you were going to be able to stay overnight at least. I know you're still on leave.' She gave the boy's unhappy face a searching glance, and it told her everything. She took him to one side. 'She's been through quite an ordeal,' she told him with compassion. 'Give her time, she'll be her old self soon enough.'

And, mildly comforted, Chuck had made some tentative arrangement to come back in a few days. On leaving, he had given Belinda a brief hug which she had returned in a half-hearted way that did nothing however to ease his disquiet. He told her that if there was anything he could do for her, she was to give the company a buzz on the radio. She had allowed him to hold her close again before take-off, finding a minor solace in his embrace, but her eyes had been close to brimming over when she had involuntarily recalled the magic of that other man's touch.

It had taken only a short time for her to decide that the best antidote was to plunge straight back into work. Her time in Canada was nearly up and there was still work to be done.

The next few days were busy with the sound of the cassette recorder as she played and re-played the tapes, trying to document the main features as outlined by Derek in his assignment briefing. It was a peculiar form of self-torture, she decided, to play so often the particular tapes that contained recordings of a certain voice, and once she had been so overcome with grief and longing when she heard the familiar tones that she had picked up the recorder in both hands and had been about to hurl it despairingly at the wall, when the calm voice of reason had warned her in no uncertain terms of the futility of such behaviour.

'Oh, help me, someone!' she had sobbed into her coverlet that night. 'Please cure me of this futile longing for someone who can never be mine.'

If Mrs Mac had noticed the puffiness of eyes spending too much time in weeping, she said nothing, but her kindly face had a troubled look which was difficult to conceal. Gently she had probed Belinda to try to discover what had taken place in the snow in her few days of physical ordeal, but the girl's replies had been evasive and Mrs Mac had had to resort to putting two and two together.

After dinner one evening, she casually introduced Barron's name into the conversation. Belinda raised her pale face. 'He seems to be called Amaruq out here,' she said. With a valiant effort she tried to conceal the tremors that shook her body on saying his name out loud. She felt she could fully understand now the Eskimo's sense of the magical and powerful associations which a name could possess.

Mrs Mac thoughtfully sugared her tea. 'I asked Mac about the name-change the other day, as it happens,' she went on. 'It seems Barron, or Amaruq as everyone now seems to prefer to call him, fought off a gang of toughs who were marauding and otherwise making a nuisance of themselves up around the Hell's Gate region where the Nasaq have their summer camp.'

'A gang?' breathed Belinda, looking up sharply.

'Three or four of them, so the story goes. Two of them for sure were on the run from the Mounties, one was a well-known bad lot from Invik, and the fourth—well, it seems he was an Eskimo who'd been thrown out from his tribe and bore a grudge against the Nasaq in particular. One of them was apparently killed in the fracas, and the others were eventually pulled in by the police. It was all quite hush-hush. The Nasaq kept themselves to themselves anyway, and when the story leaked out to the other tribes there were such scenes of jubilation, Mac says it would have been more than a white man's skin was worth if he'd tried to step in and lay the blame on any one man.'

'And that man was Amaruq?'

Belinda took the new revelation calmly. It only confirmed something she had known in the deepest recess of her heart for a long time, but it did nothing to alleviate the pain of her present half-life.

All the work she could reasonably cope with alone was drawing to an end and she knew that it would soon be time to say goodbye to the Macs and return to England. She had made no plans to see Chuck and she dreaded the thought of having to fly back to Invik with him. If things had been different, if her emotions hadn't been exploded in all directions by her unforeseen encounter with a man like Amaruq, she knew she could have happily included Chuck in her life's pattern. But that something totally unexpected and out of this world, which she had idly put forward in her earlier musings on the possible reasons for choosing the harsh and primitive way of the Arctic in preference to big city life, had actually happened to her. And it made the undemanding love of a young daredevil like Chuck seem like a great irrelevance. Once scorched by the fires of real passion, no pale substitute would fill its place.

She had already started to pack her files and tapes and there were just one or two things which she had not been able to make out that were left as a final task. Fathom how she would, she could not make head nor tail of some of the words on one of the tapes. It was the drum dance sequence, when the sound levels had been all to pot—

there were two songs which were relatively easy to note down, but then the sound of the drum rose to an excited frenzy and the words petered out beneath it. Just hearing it again brought a lump into Belinda's throat, but she steeled herself to go through with it. Somehow she felt it was important to know what the words had been, but she had almost despaired of uncovering the secret when she remembered what Amaruq had told her in the hospital. His advice had been to visit Nuallataq the shaman if she ran into difficulties.

After a few preliminary enquiries, though with a heavy heart, she had armed herself with her cassette recorder once more and set out on the snowy track to the top of the settlement where Nuallataq lived alone among the relics of his art.

It was not the first time she had visited him, but this time she had the experience of the last few weeks behind her, and she felt nervous at meeting those shrewd all-seeing eyes which had the reputation of being able to strip away the protective layer of social convention to reveal the truth lying hidden in the privacy of the heart.

As she stepped inside his house, never before had it seemed so dark and mysterious. By nature a sceptic, she could not ignore the weird power that seemed to emanate from the figure of the old man who sat motionless, back turned to her, in a corner of the room. She knew he was expecting her, but he was sitting with his face to the wall, a hood pulled over his eyes, as he emitted a weird chanting that sent shivers up and down her spine. Quietly, almost as if entering some sacred chapel, she knelt down on a caribou skin blanket placed near the door and began to spread out her notes and recording machine to wait for him to finish.

Eventually the chant slowed and with a slight pause before turning he said her name once, sharply. Belinda held her breath. As the sound faded she imagined it took on the timbre of Amaruq's voice, the quality and tone of it. She brushed her hair back angrily. She must really have got it bad, to be so smitten that she was even hearing his voice! She held her breath as Nuallataq turned to look at her.

There was nothing but twinkling kindness in his eyes as she falteringly told him of her present difficulty in making out some of the words on the drum dance tape. Without speaking, he gestured to the tape to have it switched on. Belinda pressed the button and once again the throbbing of the drum rang out. The sound seemed to fill the little hut, bringing it alive with the sounds of the past, and when they eventually faded and the tape had clicked to a stop, Nuallataq leaned forward with a wicked smile.

'Magic, isn't it?' He spoke rapid, strongly inflected English that was difficult to follow at first. Now he was grinning up at the girl. 'White man's magic to separate the sound from the spirit.' He let a long slow breath empty his lungs, then he settled back more comfortably among his furs. 'This is the song of the white man Amaruq,' he said, shooting a sudden glance at her from beneath beetling brows.

'But it can't be—that's not his voice at all,' protested Belinda in puzzlement.

'His song partner is singing, because it would not do for a man to sing his own praises.' Dreamily the old shaman repeated the Eskimo words while Belinda noted them down. They made no sense to her, but that was not her concern. All Derek had told her to do was to make phonetic notations of anything she couldn't understand.

When the old man had finished he bowed his head. Feeling that this was a sign that he wanted her to leave, she started to pack away her things into the holdall. When she had finished she rose to leave, but he looked up at her and held up his hand.

'To make separations is sometimes the way to survive,' he told her, 'otherwise there is no practical purpose for such behaviour. Everything is one.' After uttering these words he closed his eyes and seemed to go into a trance, and Belinda crept out of the hut as silently as she could.

All the way back to the house she pondered over Nuallataq's cryptic words. Probably in accordance with his allotted role he felt he had to deliver this kind of apparently significant lesson, it would be expected of a man in his position, but Belinda had the strange feeling that there was something else behind his words, something she could not quite lay a finger on.

When she got to the house she became aware of a familiar figure shrouded in outdoor furs standing in the kitchen, and when he turned she saw it was Taqaq, fresh from his visit to his people up at Sanderson's place. She greeted him warmly, giving him a sisterly hug and en-quiring after his doings with interest. He told her things had gone well, that he had got married to the girl, and had left her temporarily with his own people while he came to Two Rivers. Somehow his presence seemed to ease her inner pain a little, as if his recent proximity to Amaruq, if a separation of fifty or sixty miles of barren snow could be called that, was some how capable of bringing Amaruq himself that little bit closer. She care-fully skirted any mention of his name, however, and Taqaq seemed too busy telling her about his new wife and his plans for the future to seem to want to know more than the barest details of what had befallen her after he left her with Amaruq in the snow house.

'I'm here to take delivery of a snowmobile,' he told her. 'It's time modern technology was introduced up there. They make hard work for themselves. I'm also in business as a messenger,' he added with a slightly mysteri-ous look in his eyes. 'Anybody got any messages they want taking back?' He looked expectantly at her, but as if she hadn't heard, she was already across the kitchen to the door leading into the hall. Her face held no particular expression when she said to him, 'I'll just dump my tape recorder in my room, then I'll join you again and you can tell me more about this snowmobile.'

Once in the privacy of her room she quickly emptied the holdall of its contents, placing the recorder in its now accustomed place on the pine table. She located the correct file for the drum dance notes and was just about to put the afternoon's phonetic transcription of Amaruq's song into it, when she paused. The notation made no sense to her yet, but if she tried she could pick out odd words here and there. She peered closer—*nanuq* was a word repeated several times. So it was something about a polar bear. What she had expected, it would be a hunting song of some sort. She scanned the page for other familiar sounds, but it was no good. If she wanted to know more she would have to do some work on it. Perhaps she would have a proper look later on. Here would be her final link with Amaruq. The song would tell her some of the things he had been reluctant to reveal to her. Who knew, it might even give some clue about his mysterious past, before he came to live among the Eskimo. On another impulse Belinda felt like tearing the sheet of paper into shreds. What did it matter now what she learned about him? It would be just another sharp turn of the knife. She brushed her hair before going down again.

There was an air of excitement in the room as she came in. Mrs Mac looked up with a smile. 'Ikluk's just had a little boy!' she called out above the hum of conversation. Mac was already opening a celebration bottle and handed Belinda a glass. It was as if her world had fallen apart. Although it was something she knew was soon to happen, to experience the fact that the man she loved was now a father was something that drained the colour from her cheeks and made her heart pound suffocatingly. As if in a dream she endured the conversation of her companions, but eventually she could take no more. With a feeble excuse she left the room and half ran, half stumbled across the hall towards her own room. As she reached her door she heard Taqaq's voice behind her.

'Belinda,' he called. 'Wait a moment!' Blinking back the tears, she turned to him, wanting nothing more than the privacy of her own room and the darkness where she could hide in pain. He came up to her. 'I shall be leaving early tomorrow morning,' he told her.

'I'm sorry,' she broke out. 'I feel dreadful—a headache. I'm sorry we haven't had much of a chat.'

'I'm sorry too,' he rejoined. 'By the time I return in the spring you will be in England, yes?'

'I guess so.' Belinda tried to smile, but her face felt stiff with unshed tears.

'I meant what I said to you earlier,' he went on. 'I'm here to be a messenger if you want me. Amaruq is working his traplines only fifty miles or so from where my people live.'

Belinda touched him briefly on the arm. 'No message,' she said. 'I'm sure there'll be more important news to take back to him than anything I can possibly say.' Taqaq looked strangely at her for a moment. Not trusting herself to control the tears that threatened, she pushed open the door of her room. 'Goodbye, Taqaq. Thank you for your help. Perhaps we'll meet again.'

She stood for a long moment with her back against the door. In the distance she could hear the hum of conversation and sudden bursts of laughter, but her own room was silent with the kind of silence that only emphasised the emptiness she felt inside. She flung herself into bed and lay for a long time tossing and turning, listening first to the gradual fading of the talk in the room below, then to the sound of people walking away from the building, and finally to the only sound that was left, the night wind as it howled yearningly through the copse of sitka pines.

The night seemed full of silence now. Belinda listened for as long as she could before flinging herself out of bed with a sigh of exasperation. Wakefully she paced back and forth across the room. There seemed to be nothing that would make her sleep. With a final sigh she let herself be drawn towards the file on her work table. 'All right,' she told herself angrily, 'so be it. One more turn of the knife. I may as well translate the damn song and get it over with. Anything's better than lying here, torturing myself with the way he looks, the sound of his voice. I'll translate it. Then it will be well and truly the end. I absolutely refuse to give another thought to him after tonight.'

With that she opened the file, took out her pen, and began to read. It was towards dawn by the time she had managed to work her way through the piece. Because there were three parts to most words, a stem, a suffix and the grammatical termination, she had started to list them in three separate books. It meant that she had to look each word up three times before she could begin to make any sense of it. As she had guessed, it was a hunting song, but there was more to it than that. It now told how Amaruq and his joking-brother—yet another structural relationship, she noted—had been hunting out on the ice floes in early spring when they had surprised a polar bear in its birthing den. Before they could retreat the huge beast had come charging out at them bowling over the dogs, and smashing the sled. Amaruq had fallen and the bear, picking him as her victim, had turned with a roar to the attack. The other man had dropped his gun in the confusion and was unable to fire, but with no thought for his own safety he had thrown himself between the bear and Amaruq, armed only with a short knife. This had given Amaruq time to fire his gun and he had felled the bear with one shot straight between the eyes. The tragedy of the story was that Amaruq's companion had suffered horrifying abdominal wounds, and although Amaruq had driven the dogs non-stop for over twenty-four hours in the hastily repaired sled, his hunting companion, a man called Intuq, had died from internal bleeding only five miles from the trading post.

Belinda's face showed conflicting emotions as she read through these words, and, oblivious to the fact that the settlement was now already beginning to come to life with the onset of morning, she set about translating the last few lines with fierce concentration. Eventually her task was finished. It was already breakfast time. But she sat back as if to take in the full impact of what she now read. For a long time she did nothing but look at the words she had written. Then she sprang into action.

This time, if there were tears they were not tears of grief.

In a moment or two she was making for the door, the translation clutched in her hand. She was sure there were no mistakes. Carefully she had checked the last part of the story.

It told how, in a desperate race against time, Amaruq had driven the sled with its wounded man across the ice towards help, and how the dying man, realising that the end was near, told Amaruq that his wife was to have a child, and how Amaruq had made a promise to care for his wife and child, to find the wife a new husband when the period of mourning was over, and how the child would ensure that the memory of his father's bravery would never die. Tears of relief and sorrow, and a mixture of many other emotions, coursed down Belinda's cheeks as she pulled on her jacket. In no time she was at the door of Taqaq's lodging.

By the look on his face he had been expecting something like this, for she had scarcely set foot inside before he had told her precisely when he expected to reach the traplines at Sandersons and how long it would take before someone could get back to the settlement.

'Of course,' he added with a grin, 'if that someone travelled back by snowmobile, just supposing they managed to get hold of one, it would take only two sleeps at most.'

Belinda hugged him impulsively, a cry of relief quickly superseded by a look of apprehension. 'That presupposes that anyone would want to get back here in that much of a hurry,' she said.

The next two days dragged by in an agony of slowness. Chuck's plane was due to alight on the little landing strip

ready to fly her out of the settlement early on the third
morning, allowing her enough time to catch the daily
scheduled flight from Paulatuk, to arrive in Toronto in
the early evening of the same day. But it was the narrow
track curling round the edge of the lake and out into the
tundra beyond the settlement and not the strip to which
Belinda's eyes continually strayed. She could find no way
of stopping herself from again and again wandering over
to the window at the front of the post-house to gaze out
with eyes dark with yearning for a sign of any new arrival
at the camp.

Already snow was encrusted thickly round the eaves of
the timber-framed building and for the last few days a
biting wind had swept mercilessly and undeviatingly from
the northern ice fields. Belinda's heart too felt as if swept
by an icy wind, made cold with the dead fear of a longing
which she dared not voice. Was she being foolish to expect
anything from Amaruq now, after the way she had treated
him? Had she made the urgency of her message via Taqaq
as crystal clear as she might? Or would he push it to the
back of his mind and only bring it up in casual conversation months later when she was already back in England,
brokenhearted over the loss of her love? She shuddered. A
future without Amaruq was impossible to contemplate.
Again she went to the window, gripping the sill until her
knuckles showed white. But again the track was bare of
all human life and only the wild flurries of snow gave any
movement to the desolate scene.

'Well,' said Mrs Mac, breaking into her thoughts late
on the second morning as she stood for the hundredth
time at the window, 'how's the packing coming along?'
She paused and eyed the hollow-cheeked girl with pensive
glance. The child looked lovelorn if she was any judge,
and Mrs Mac knitted her brow with concern. She had
always thought Amaruq strange and unpredictable and
she found it difficult to fathom why a nice girl like Belinda
should be so foolhardy as to fall for a man whose very

glance seemed to spell danger. She sighed. It was lucky
the child was going back to England the next day. No
doubt she would soon forget her infatuation for such an
unsuitable mate. Belinda turned pained eyes towards the
older woman.

'If someone travelled back from—from . . .' the name
died on her lips. She tried again. 'Taqaq said it would
only take two sleeps at most——' but again her voice
tailed away.

Mrs Mac put an arm round her shoulders. 'You have a
long journey ahead of you,' she said, hugging the girl
impulsively. 'Soon you'll be back in your old life with all
your friends, your work. Think of the future, not the
past.'

Belinda smiled wanly. 'I suppose you're right.'

She knew though, deep in her heart, that the prospect
of her old life, now that she had known the passion of real
love, was as desolate as the scene outside the window. In
despair she glanced one last time through the snow-en-
crusted glass. So used to the empty track was she that at
first her glance failed to take in the speck of a figure almost
obscured by the scudding snow flurries. With a start she
glanced back, peering more carefully through the window.
'Look——' she breathed, then more excitedly she turned
to Mrs Mac, gripping her tightly by the arm and dragging
her towards the window. 'Do you see someone?' she
breathed, half dead with expectancy. 'Look, there! Coming
up the track——' It was impossible to see who it was, but
there was something familiar about the stance of the figure
in the snowmobile so that even though she was at the
same time telling herself not to be foolish, another more
exultant voice was beginning to shout on a rising tide of
certainty.

'It looks like a snowmobile,' said Mrs Mac when at last
she had managed to make out the tiny figure fast approaching the settlement. She turned to the girl. But
Belinda was not waiting for further discussion. Snatching

her furs from the door-hook, she was already half into
them and scrambling into her fur boots before Mrs Mac
could put any further questions. With one word on her
lips she was outside, stumbling and slipping in the drifts
of new snow, unheeding now the cold and the sharp wind
which was flinging bursts of snow into her face in joyful
flurries.

Half-way down the track the driver of the snowmobile
and Belinda came face to face. With a final roar the driver
cut the engine and the machine came scudding to a halt
in front of her. In the sudden silence that followed only
the patter of snow granules could be heard striking their
hoods like hard grains of rice, then the moment's silence
was broken by one gruff word as the driver climbed swiftly
down. 'Darling!' With one movement he had swept the
girl into his arms, pressing his lips urgently against her
cheek, searching out the warmth in her softly yielding
lips.

At last, breathless, he held her at arm's length and let
his eyes take in her tousled hair where her hood had fallen
back and her shining eyes seemed to answer his in a look
that swept away all the previous weeks of uncertainty. To
Belinda it seemed as if her legs had turned to water and
she hung weakly within the safety of his encircling arms
as he tilted her lips to his once again. She gazed adoringly
into his eyes as she told him in a faltering voice how Taqaq
had said it would take two sleeps at most to get back to
the settlement.

'Two sleeps?' smiled Amaruq tenderly. 'As if I'd waste
time sleeping when I could be travelling back to you!' He
hugged her close again. 'Why did you leave it so late?' he
murmured between kisses. 'What made you change your
mind about me?'

'I translated your drum song,' she faltered.

He pulled her close against his muscular chest, snow
covered his fur parka, and his face was like ice as he
pressed it close again on her warm skin. For a long time

they stood encircled in each other's arms as if never to be parted, then Barron pushed her hair back from her flushed face and looked long and deeply into her smiling eyes. 'And that made such a difference?' he asked.

'If only you'd told me there was nothing between you and Ikluk,' she said at last by way of explanation. 'I thought she was your woman, bearing your child——' She buried her face against his shoulder as relief at seeing him and being at last in his arms engulfed her.

'To come so close to losing you——' he murmured huskily, burying his face in her hair. 'I could never understand what was wrong. I'd no idea thoughts like that were going through your mind, my love.' He held her tighter. 'It seemed as if you were deliberately trying to drive me out of my mind—the look in your eyes seemed to say you wanted me, but whenever I tried to get close, you fought me off like a wildcat. I was in a turmoil of indecision. Promise me one thing, darling,' he bent to kiss her yet again, 'promise me that you'll never let unspoken worries come between us again.' His strong face looked pale and vulnerable as his eyes searched hers for reassurance.

'I promise,' she said simply, 'but only if you promise to take me with you wherever you go, even if I do happen to pass out if there's a bit of a blizzard.'

'I'll never let that happen again,' he vowed, pressing her close again. 'My trapline days are over.'

Belinda opened her eyes wide.

'I never did explain what I was doing out here, did I?' His lips curved in a wry smile. 'I'm afraid I have a confession to make.' He glanced apprehensively at the girl in his arms and Belinda in her turn felt a quiver of fear at the thought that all the rumours about his disreputable past were to be proved. 'Perhaps I was just playing at Eskimos, like you said. Though four years is a long time to play——' he hesitated.

'Go on,' she urged in a low voice.

'Well, I happen to have a foot in the academic camp like you,' he shrugged almost apologetically. 'Before I came out here I was a junior lecturer in philology.'

She heaved a sigh of relief. 'Is that what your skeleton in the cupboard boils down to?' she grinned.

'That's not all,' he broke in. She felt his hold on her tighten and his lips hardened for a moment. 'There was a reason for my opting out of that life—a good reason. Or so I thought. Maybe even now——' he looked at her suddenly with that appraising glance which seemed to strip her and penetrate to the very heart of her being. 'No!' He gave a short laugh and the tension seemed to vanish in an instant from around his lips and eyes. 'I haven't travelled a day and a night through an Arctic blizzard to throw away the prize at the end of it all. There might have been a reason for opting out—but there's every reason in the world for opting in again. That's if you'll have me?'

Belinda hugged him closer as if to say could there be any doubt. 'But you're still being mysterious about your past. Not that it matters. Just so long as I'm here in your arms.'

He kissed her lightly on the forehead. 'You have a right to have your questions answered,' he told her. 'I'm not being deliberately secretive. It's just that I find it difficult to talk about that time now. It all seems so long ago. I'll tell you what happened. It was like this. While I was out here, doing research in the summer vacation, some discrepancies were discovered in the departmental accounts and I was accused of embezzlement. Falsely, I might add——'

'You've no need to tell me that,' she broke in softly, hugging him closer.

'Luckily the truth finally came out, but not before several months had elapsed. I was so disgusted with the way the newspapers blew the whole thing up into a major academic scandal that I decided to stay out here. To tell

you the truth, I didn't know where to go. I'd been sus-
pended from my job. There was really nothing and no
one by that time—to go back to.' For a moment his eyes
clouded. 'I admit I felt very bitter that no one stood by
me. For a long time I just wanted to cut myself off from
white people. It seemed as if they were all the same—
thoroughly corrupted by modern civilisation. I'd also
grown to love and respect the people here.'

He touched the jacket she was wearing. 'This was one
of the furs Ikluk's husband and I were bringing back with
us when that terrible thing happened.' He bent to kiss her
gently on the lips. 'It seems right that you should have it.'
For a moment they clung together. When he released her
there was a sign of the old devilish gleam in his eyes.
'That's all in the past. There's the future to think of now.
What I'd like to do is marry you and take you home to
England, but not necessarily in that order.' He paused.
'I've been offered the chance to go back and do research
in my old department. They've been making overtures
for some time and have awarded me quite a lot of money
for the work I've done so far. Perhaps now's the time to
take them up on their offer before they change their
minds. When I finally publish I should have quite a
tidy income one way or another.' A quizzical gleam came
into his eyes. 'I shall have to start looking for a research
assistant too, as soon as I get back. That's if I can find
anyone well enough up in Eskimo affairs to be of any use.'
He gave a wolfish grin. 'I suppose I shall have the chore of
interviewing scores of ambitious young men for the job.'

'Or perhaps just one ambitious young woman?' asked
Belinda, with a mischievous look.

He paused, a softening in his usually piercing glance.
'I take that to mean that you might feel like throwing in
your lot with an old fur-trapper after all?'

'Describe paradise to me,' she murmured. 'It's the same
thing.'

They had both boarded the plane a few days later on the first leg of their journey home. There had only been Chuck to face. But when he saw Belinda's shining eyes and Barron's arm protectively around her, there was no need for explanations. 'You win some, you lose some,' he'd grinned, and cuffed Barron on the shoulder. 'I guess we've more in common than I realised.' And as they climbed down out of the plane later that morning, he went up to Barron. 'Keep on making her happy,' he said.

'I will, or perish in the attempt,' replied Barron, a smile breaking across his face.

Now Belinda raised her lips to be kissed, oblivious to the bustle of the crowd in the departure lounge of the main airport in Toronto. Barron's arms were tight around her waist, and, after the heady rapture as his lips brushed hers, they walked like that towards the aircraft which was going to take them at last into a new life together.

Harlequin Plus
THE SHAMAN OF THE INUIT

The flat Arctic tundra rolls away into the horizon in shades of dark green and brown. A small band of Inuit (Eskimos) are gathered around the *inukshuk*, a tall marker made of stones indicating that the caribou pass by here on their annual migration. But now which way do the Inuit go in search of the herds? It is cold, and already a few snowflakes dance in the frosty air. They turn to their shaman for direction.

The shaman, or *angatkut*, walks a short distance away and sits at a place where there are no footprints. He draws his hood up over his head, closes his eyes and waits for his helping spirits to bring him a vision from Pinga, the great goddess who dwells in the sky.

This man became a shaman many years earlier when his dreams told him that Pinga had chosen him. Since wisdom is found only through suffering and solitude, the shaman exposed himself to loneliness, great cold and hunger for many weeks, till Hila, "the goddess of everything feared in the air," noticed him and gave him his visions and guiding spirits.

The shaman is very important to the Inuit because he or she—for a woman can be a shaman, too—is both priest and doctor. As well as healing and protecting people from evil, the shaman is also skilled in magic. He is, above all, a medium of communication between the Inuit and the spirit world.

While the other Inuit are chanting softly a short way off, the shaman is still squatting by himself. Then he stirs. A spirit has descended from Pinga and is speaking to him. He sees clearly the road his people must travel. The Inuit watching him see him smile and open his eyes. They begin to smile, too. Pinga has been good to them, and now they know they will find the caribou, and their people will eat through this long winter ahead.